A Time Traveler's Journal

To Bonnie —

May time's
enfoldment be a

blessing to you!

Stanton dall

A Time Traveler's Journal

Stanton Call

Yazdan Publishing

A Time Traveler's Journal

Yazdan Publishing First Printing, April 2022

Printed in the United States of America

ISBN-13: 978-1-938838-08-8

Yazdan Publishing
P O Box 56545
Virginia Beach, VA 23456

To Carol and Lindy,
who journeyed with Ben from the very first,

and in appreciation of George Peabody (1795-1869),
Manuela Sáenz (1797-1856),
Emanuel Swedenborg (1688-1772),
and Marie Louise Habets (1905-1986)
for their part in it.

I am fairly certain that any amount of reason will make this tale difficult to believe but I assure you it has been my experience of truth. I may not be certain that it is true with the same level of certainty that December 25 is Christmas, or that spring comes every March in the northern hemisphere, or that the earth rotates around the sun, but I can tell you that it is true to the extent that it has certainly appeared to be my experience.

For some time now, I have perceived the story I am about to describe with my own eyes; I have lived it with what might be called personal familiarity; and, I have felt it to the very depths of my being.

As to whether or not you will accept this as "truth" in your own consciousness will be entirely up to you. It is yours to decide if it is true in the truest sense of the word – true beyond even the illusion of space and time.

Ben #239, recruit

Obviously, that which is of the utmost importance isn't why or even how the decision was made by the Core to induct a trainee into the League. The focal point for each recruit is instead WHAT – WHAT is it that YOU bring to the Time Traveler's League and when does that WHAT become most necessary in maintaining the sanctity of a timeline?

Ultimately, the purpose for each and every recruit is to preserve the Akasha and the time-space illusion that guides the throngs of humankind along individualized paths of consciousness growth. That intention has guided the League ever since – what has come to be called – "Moment One" first entered the Collective Illusion.

Excerpt, "Introduction Orientation," *A Time Traveler's Code of Conduct* **by Ruth #7**

ONE: Journal Entry – March 15 ATL

I am a time traveler. I have to admit that the phrase used to sound unusual to me, but no more. It is who I am now. It is how I spend my time of late. It is what I do. I am a time traveler, or if you prefer the term, a "Wayfarer." This has become the path of my existence.

I have not always been a time traveler but I have always possessed the ability to relate to and interact with all kinds of people. Truly, I have some measure of skill and experience with diplomacy. It is a forte. Although it has never been clearly stated by any member of "the League," or even by the Core which governs it, I do believe that diplomacy is the reason I first came to their attention. If not the main reason, it is certainly a reason. Ultimately, my work with diplomacy led to my being pursued as a recruit. I know that both Milton #71, my direct supervisor, and Sara #11, who is Governor-General of the entire Core, have already found reason to compliment my work in this regard.

The League? I refer to the League of Time Travelers. Yes, I am one among many time travelers. On occasion, I have been called recruit #239; although it has never been made clear as to the method in which these numbers are assigned. For that reason, I have no idea how many of us may be similarly employed. Perhaps it is not mine to know. I do imagine that there are hundreds working in said profession. Personally, since my arrival, I have come to know more than a dozen such individuals like myself. Certainly, there appears to be sufficient work to remain industrious and to keep oneself occupied. As to how it became my profession, I should probably start with the day I died, for it was at my death that my personal adventure with time, and the management thereof, actually began.

From the outset, let me affirm that death is truly misunderstood. Even that statement, however, forms all manner of misconceptions to the untrained. Perhaps I should instead establish as a foundation the fact that consciousness seemingly exists whether in death, or in life, or in any movement through space and time. Death in one realm is simply birth into another. However, I certainly do not recommend hastening the experience.

Yes, there seem to be many timelines. I, myself, have had to dabble in three or four while rectifying the very same experience. One certainly considers one's actions to be an industrious pursuit when they lead to the appropriate course of history. The Core has labeled the authorized version of *THE TIMELINE* we constantly endeavor to maintain as the "approved timeline" – or

ATL for short. To be sure, I once believed that time flowed like a river from point A to point B and then to point C, and so forth. Unfortunately, I have come to understand that it absolutely does not unfold in such an orderly fashion, and the involvement of those who would bend time for their own amusement or personal gain only further complicates the work of the League.

The day that I died was unlike anything I might have imagined. I must admit that I had long prepared for the adventure as I was in the main confined to my chamber, bedridden and ill for more than a year. To be sure, I was aged by any measure of the day. In later life, I had often taken to a gourmand's palate, and admittedly I possessed a lifelong fondness of tippling – both of which led to more than a decade of arthritic gout. To be sure, these things have a bearing upon the composition of a man's wellbeing. I had such a passion for food, and drink, and the adoration of more than an occasional woman, that my body simply wore itself out. Although I should note that my mind, which rarely gave in to moderate use, retained its vigor up until the end.

The day of my departure from this mortal coil was as normal as these departures tend to be in all respects but one: it would be the occasion of my recruitment. In the main, it would not stand out for any other reason. Of course, my body was wracked with pain, my extremities were swollen as if they were about to burst, and my every breath was a struggle. As an octogenarian several years over I had grown used to such inevitable irritants. What I did not fathom at the time was that death has often been used by the Core as the vehicle for one's recruitment. After all, it leaves so few loose ends or unanswered questions as to one's whereabouts.

For several hours, my grandsons had been dutifully standing guard and had only departed momentarily to take some sustenance of soup, bread, and butter. It was while they were elsewhere employed that the fogginess in my mind suddenly departed and some semblance of consciousness returned. As my eyes regained their focus, I became aware of a comely lass near my bedside. She appeared to be near to the age of 20. She smiled and spoke:

"My name is Ruth."

Not having verbalized anything for quite some time, I was less than certain that I still retained the capacity for coherent speech but, nonetheless, words did manage to come to me: "Dear Child, I would rise to greet thee but my malady confines me thusly."

Her response surprised me greatly, "I have come to offer you a position."

I found myself chuckling at the thought, "Unless you require the skills of a sluggard, I will be of no use to you. I have seen 80 years and can no longer claim to be the man of my youth."

The smile on the lass widened, "I am far older than you . . . far, far older indeed. "

I looked in disbelief and squinted my eyes to affirm that a young woman did, in fact, stand beside me. "May I ask, how old?"

"I will only say that even while your grandfather's grandfather walked the earth, I would have considered quite aged."

"How can you appear thusly?"

"I am a member of the League – we manage our appearance and time. Should you choose to be employed in a selfsame manner, I offer you this."

She extended one arm and opened her hand to display a pocket watch that at first glance seemed common in appearance but upon closer inspection was quite detailed in design.

"A watch?"

"We call it a Horologium," she replied with certainty, and then added with complete sincerity, "Rather than simply keeping track of the time, it has the capacity to manage it."

The idea certainly intrigued me.

"If you choose to take this from me, your new journey will begin immediately." She nodded with confidence and went to place the Horologium within my hand.

"What of my grandsons?"

She was matter-of-fact, "They will bury their grandfather, and you will be shown the path of a Wayfarer. But it is a choice you must make quickly."

Well, what was I to do? If such a decision had been yours to pursue – to follow after an attractive young woman to parts unknown or to struggle with one's final breath until the very end, only to find oneself then standing before the Maker of the Universe – what choice would you have made? Naturally, I took the watch.

I remember opening my hand to accept the Horologium but admittedly much of what followed seems unclear to me. I do know that I finally became conscious of sitting at a student's wooden desk in some semblance of a small classroom with four others in rapt attention. Although they were much younger, each of the four appeared to suffer some measure of confusion just as myself.

Standing at the front of the room with a desk and a large whiteboard on the wall behind her was a dark-skinned matronly (although not unattractive) woman. I assumed her to be some semblance of teacher, as upon her desk had been stacked a half dozen white texts. She held a stylus in her hand, which she wove about for emphasis whenever she spoke, beginning even with the introduction of herself: "You may call me, Agnes #23."

As we all sat there in amazement and wonderment, she proceeded to introduce us one to another. There was an attentive-looking Swede whom she called "Emanuel #41." As I could not fathom the possibility that there were forty others named "Emanuel" lurking somewhere nearby, I quickly assumed that this was the forty-first individual to find himself in this particular locale. That notion was quickly discarded, however, when she pointed in my direction and introduced me as "Ben #239."

As the others turned to glance in my direction, my hand rose in acknowledgment. I could not help but notice that the aged fingers of the octogenarian had been left behind and replaced instead with the palm of my youth. I had hardly time to ponder such a marvelous change when the instructress turned to the next individual, a dark-haired Latin woman, whom she called "Manuela #64." Then came "George #111" (who possessed the visage and attire of a young banker), and finally a calm, French lass she referred to as "Bonne Soeur Marie #304." After each of us had been introduced, I found myself turning once again to my hands to contemplate their youthful appearance. I suddenly remembered the Horologium and wondered as to its whereabouts.

"Each of your personal recruiters will have placed the Horologium safely inside a pocket," Agnes replied to no one in particular and then waved the stylus at each of us, "These are issued by the ATL Mission Office and you are responsible for them at all times. They are not to leave your possession!"

I found the Horologium inside the pocket of my shirt – although it was a shirt I had never before seen – and then quickly redirected my attention back to our teacher at the front of the room.

"Welcome to the first class of your induction into the League. If you only remember one thing from this instruction let it be the understanding that there is only one moment in time and that one moment has limitless manifestations."

I pondered the full meaning of such an idea as she repeated herself.

"There is ONE moment in time, with limitless manifestations!" The stylus whipped through the air before her, as if she hoped to underscore the statement. "The only time is NOW, but our individual perception of that NOW is without parameters."

"Is time not sequential?" George pondered aloud. "Can it not be counted?" Surely this was the verbalization of a banker.

"Let us turn to our text for further clarity," came the response. Agnes proceeded to take the stack of texts, passing one book to each of the students, while retaining one for herself.

The title was certainly intriguing, *A Time Traveler's Code of Conduct,*" and as the author's name jumped out at me, I caught my breath: "Ruth #7!" Was this the very Ruth who had entered my bedchamber earlier that selfsame day? Before I had firmly resolved to ask that question aloud, Agnes encouraged the class, "Let's turn to Chapter Three on page 51. Ben, could you read the chapter title and first paragraph for us?"

I followed her direction and read the title, "The Limitless Expression of Time," and then proceeded with the first paragraph: "Start with Moment One. Multiply that moment by every individual who has ever walked the earth. Next, multiply that sum by every day each of those individuals has ever lived, and include the calculations for every possible choice and every possible relationship and every possible action for each of those individuals for every single moment of their lives. Then take into account the fact that each of these innumerable possibilities is happening exactly NOW. Only then will you begin to have some semblance of the enormity of the task we manage and the multitude of potential timelines with which you will find yourself involved."

As the words were completed, I desired to reread them with the hope of finding some degree of additional clarity, but Agnes proceeded to the white surface behind her and drew a solitary line.

"Let us imagine that the line before us is some measurement of your current perception of time." She turned to the class momentarily and although the stylus no longer touched the whiteboard or drew a black line, she continued to wave it about before us.

"For ease of understanding, let us label each end of the line." She turned toward the wall and labeled the left end of the line 1750 and the right end 2240, and then spoke thusly for further clarification: "Let me assure you that I have not chosen these dates for any notable reason other than for additional edification. I could have decided instead to label the left side 682 and the right 9430. You might be surprised to learn that we could have done the reverse, as well, labeling the left side 9430 and the right 682, but this can be covered in a later class. For right now, let us imagine this one illustration is simply the collective perception of linear time."

"But," she emphasized, pointing the ever-moving stylus at us as she spoke, "what if time is not linear?"

Her speech paused but she continued to move

about with more enthusiasm than seemed required for the situation. I began to ponder whether this woman standing before us had some degree of theatrical training.

"I want you to imagine instead that we rotate this line on its existing axis exactly 90 degrees to the right – I could have chosen the left but either way matters not. How does the picture of our line now appear?"

Immediately, Bonne Soeur Marie #304 raised her hand excitedly and responded in French, "C'est une pointe," before repeating herself in English, "It is a point . . . a dot."

"Exactly," Agnes and her stylus bobbed in agreement. "All of the dates that we might have written on our line are now contained within one solitary point, one moment in time, one NOW. That is the ultimate nature of time."

"And if that is the case," Agnes continued, "and I assure you that it is – what is creating the general perception of time that the masses continue to embrace?"

Emanuel was the first to speak, "The primary properties of the physical world are space and time, but I do not believe these are properties in the eternal."

"They are not," Agnes agreed, "but I assure you they are only properties in the physical world because of the belief that it is so. Anyone else?"

Other hands in the classroom began to wave about, and it seemed only appropriate that I should choose to express my own desire for participation. I raised a youthful hand, prompting Agnes to point the stylus in my direction.

I pondered aloud, "Perhaps we fool ourselves with some measure of personal consciousness – a belief that we have chosen to embrace? Perhaps it is a shared illusion of some manner?"

"Precisely!" came her animated reply. "From the moment a child is born that child is greeted and governed by a shared deception within physical consciousness that does not exist beyond the Collective Illusion."

Gauging by the look of wonderment upon his face, George #111 appeared to be ruminating as to how counting might eventually fit into the mix after all.

Agnes continued: "Imagine the difficulty each child faces trying to overcome the illusion of time when from the very first that child is presented with the perceived notion that everything follows a particular schedule. There is a time for birth; there is a time for death." (Those words caused her to eye us all closely, as each undoubtedly had some recent familiarity with the concept.) "There is a time to get up; there is a time to go to bed. There is a time for work; there is a time for play. The dates on a calendar are thought to contain some measure of meaning. There is a time to celebrate birthdays and holidays, and beginnings and ends. All of humankind is caught up in a nonsensical measurement directing the course of their lives!" Her words were spoken with such enthusiastic zeal, I grew concerned that the stylus was near unto being thrown from her hand. "And it is this illusion each of you will learn to conquer."

Agnes stopped speaking, taking time to ascertain what level of confusion appeared on the faces before her. As I had often been guided by healthy measures of both curiosity and skepticism, I was contemplating whether it would be most illuminating to verbalize a question seeking further elucidation or request instead that we return to the text. My own love for books had effectively prompted me to suggest additional reading when Agnes led us instead toward a different course of action.

"We will resume this discussion later. For now, I would like to give you a brief introduction regarding the workings of your Horologium. If you would please take it out for closer inspection." At long last, Agnes placed the stylus upon her desk and removed her own Horologium from a dress pocket. She held it up for the class to see, waiting for each of us to do likewise.

I eagerly followed her request, wishing to know more about the mechanism that had been placed into my safekeeping. The device itself seemed to be fashioned of an extremely heavy metal with which I was not familiar. The front cover was emblazoned with the Roman numerals I through XII, entirely like the face of a grandfather clock. The back cover was etched with the lettering, "Ben #239." I nodded approvingly.

Agnes waited until each of the five of us held the object within our hands, and then pointed out the clasp that protruded from one side. "If you would each push the clasp, we can examine the inside and I will give you a basic summary of the numerous workings of the timepiece."

I followed her lead and pushed the clasp. What I saw caused me to catch my breath so completely that I remained totally unaware of anything Agnes continued to relate to the others. Within the inner face of the Horologium had been scratched the following:

Help!R7

It seemed immediately clear that wherever Ruth #7 might be, she was in desperate need of my assistance.

Beyond the astonishment of where I now found myself, and the fact that I had regained the vigor of my youthfulness, and some yet unknown circumstance surrounding Ruth #7, the rest of that first day proved uneventful. Toward the close of class, we were informed that we would have a roommate while we were taking instruction. Bonne Soeur Marie and Manuela would board together, I was partnered with George, and Emanuel was apprised that his "roomie" (as Agnes appeared extremely fond of calling these lodging arrangements) had opted not to take the Horologium when his recruiter had offered such, thus giving the Swede a room to himself.

Before we were to depart to our assigned chambers, however, I made several attempts to extract additional information from Agnes #23 about the unusual situation in which we now found ourselves. I even inquired as to the composition of the work that we might be expected to undertake. She merely responded with, "That will be covered later in the curriculum."

I wondered aloud as to how many class hours were to be a part of our overall education. "That depends," came the answer – although there came no additional illumination as to that with which the dependency was connected.

It seemed harmless enough to query as to whether or not we would have the opportunity to speak with our personal recruiters and thank them for their labors. The response was simply, "Perhaps." Obviously, this gave me no further elucidation as to how I might be of assistance to Ruth.

When I received a very stern look and no verbal response for my next question as to whether we could be provided with some clarification as to the number of time travelers currently involved in the League, it became clear that Agnes #23 had dealt with sufficient inquiries for the day. No one else moved to voice an additional thought, prompting Agnes to place the cover upon the tip of her stylus while voicing with some measure of satisfaction, "Class dismissed!"

I must confess that I liked and admired George #111 from the very commencement of our lodging arrangement. Yes, he had been a banker, and a merchant before that, and even a pauper in his youth. I came to discover that an honest reputation and an unwavering desire to help those less fortunate than himself became the hallmarks of his existence. He had even created quite a name for himself in both London and in the States and admitted to a great fondness for charity – giving money to countless individuals and causes in need.

"I found occasion to underwrite a donation fund for the impoverished of London," George revealed. "The effort became so well known that it even came to the attention of the queen."

"Queen Charlotte?" I pondered aloud.

"No, Victoria."

"I am unfamiliar with the name," I answered truthfully.

The exchange that followed made it exceedingly clear that our association with London had been separated by multiple decades. Further inquiry between us established the fact that when George was born, I had already been dead for several years.

George voiced my own opinion on the matter, "We

may find the ponderance of such things extremely confounding."

"Perhaps we must remember the line that becomes a solitary dot," came my response.

Although it was contrary to my general routine, we spoke long into the night and thereby found numerous similarities we shared. We each had a fascination with people. We were not solitary children in our youths: George was one of eight offspring; my father had sired twice that number. Each of us had enjoyed the company of a mistress (and a child as a result). George had once been engaged but never married. I had been married once and engaged on multiple occasions. We shared our biggest regret being the loss of a child. George's favorite nephew (and namesake) had died of scarlet fever; my four-year-old son had succumbed to smallpox. We each had frequently given thought to the future and imagined how we might give rise to its arrival. Truly, I enjoyed our conversation, but it seemed judicious for the present to keep the matter of the lettering scratched within my Horologium to myself.

The next morning we both confessed a desire to find ourselves involved in another stimulating classroom experience and it was not long before we were in Agnes's presence, watching her grip the stylus at the ready. After she had given us each a few moments to provide personal introductions for the rest of the class ("background information," as she chose to describe it), our instructress proceeded to write the word "Kadesh" on the board before us.

"The city of Kadesh," she said emphatically, although I assumed no one in attendance had ever heard the name of such a place spoken before. "Today, we will examine a real-world example."

"I refer to the time of Ramesses II," she said in

response to the looks of confusion which greeted her. "I want us to specifically look at the outcome in Kadesh along timelines V, XXXI, and IX." Her stylus pointed at each of us in an effort to emphasize what came next. "I want to make it entirely clear, however, that we could examine a multitude of other options but these three may be most informative for today's discussion. Let's start with IX."

Agnes wrote the Roman numerals on the board and continued. "In timeline IX, Ramesses is in the fifth year of his reign. He is a young ruler who has lost patience with the Hittite king for the Hittite's continual advances against Egypt. Ramesses decides to invade the city of Kadesh, freeing it from the occupying Hittites. *Those are the basics!*"

"What Ramesses does not know is that the Hittite king has already fortified the city. As Ramesses nears Kadesh, he will be cut off from the rest of his army and he will die in the fight that ensues, eliminating more than sixty years from his reign. Who can tell me what is problematic with this timeline?"

For a moment, there was only silence. It was George who finally chose to respond. From our conversation the night previous, I assumed his love of London libraries had led to some familiarity with the question before us.

"Ramesses II is the architect of Egypt," George responded matter-of-factly. "If Ramesses dies, the countless temples and monuments that bear witness to his rule may be no more."

Agnes nodded. "That is certainly one good answer. Even within the illusion of the twenty-first-century timeline, the monuments of Ramesses II remain the central attraction to literally millions of tourists – tourists that support the country and its 100 million inhabitants. Remove the monuments and you face the possibility of economic collapse . . . Although timeline LXI shows a much more positive outcome," she added more for herself than for anyone in attendance.

"Let us turn to timeline V," Agnes used her stylus to write the numeral on the board and then turned back toward the class. "In timeline V, on his journey to Kadesh, Ramesses captures a Hittite spy and learns that Kadesh has already been infiltrated by the Hittite army. As a result, he changes his plans and turns instead toward the Hittite capital of Tarhuntassa. In the battle that follows, much of the city is destroyed and the Hittite king is killed in the process. Who can describe the challenge with timeline V?"

I found myself dubious as to whether every book George had ever read from all the libraries in the city of London could even begin to help with the response. There was only silence. Agnes bobbed back and forth tapping a finger against the stylus as she waited patiently for someone to say something. She waited, and waited, and finally had no choice but to answer for herself:

"If the Hittite army is destroyed at this point in time, the Egyptians have yet to fully learn from the Hittite civilization how to fortify their weaponry. We must remember that the Hittites are renowned as masters of iron and metal," she added for our enlightenment. "And if the Egyptians fail to enhance their own weapons and consolidate their power, their reign upon a continent will be shortened." She looked about the class to see if anyone appeared as yet illuminated. "If the Egyptian reign is shortened, the world's discovery of mathematics and medicine will be delayed for many centuries. Obviously, this is a problem."

"That leaves timeline XXXI." Agnes drew the numerals on the board and underlined them twice for emphasis. "This timeline will be our best answer – it is, in fact, the approved timeline, which we refer to as the 'ATL.'"

She nodded in the affirmative as she turned back to the class. "In this timeline, Kadesh is still fortified by the Hittites, and Ramesses is still cut off from his army; however, in this instance rather than using his forces to attack, the idea of diplomacy suddenly enters the Pharaoh's mind, and he proposes instead a meeting with the Hittite king. Because of this outcome, in time a treaty will be proposed – the Treaty of Kadesh. This treaty will be recorded in the ATL as the first peace treaty in existence."

Agnes appeared quite satisfied with the instruction and waited to see the response of those in her charge.

Finally, it was Emanuel who found occasion to speak: "Madame Agnes, surely the acquisition of such information is necessary for us to even begin to formulate what might be an approved outcome. Is there a library or some repository of books that we might learn from beyond the confines of the class?"

"There is!" she responded with enthusiasm. "Once we have covered all of the class fundamentals, I will show you to the Akasha." Her eyes opened wide, as though on the verge of revealing some amazing secret. "You will discover that within the Akasha one can find every potential outcome that can possibly occur within space-time itself. It will take us more than a day to even begin to explore the facility."

"Señora?" Manuela #64 rose her hand to be noticed. "But how can we make certain that this timeline XXXI becomes the approved result?"

Agnes tapped her stylus four times in the air for each of the four words she spoke aloud, "We need a diplomat."

It was Bonne Soeur Marie who voiced what several

had been thinking, "Monsieur Ben!"

When everyone turned to look in my direction, I could not help myself from expressing the only words that came to mind: "There never was a good war or a bad peace."

The primary objective for each and every mission is about much more than the mission itself. Obviously, aspects of any mission can be revisited – although never in exactly the same way, for once interaction with a timeline has occurred, space-time is altered ever so slightly. What is instead paramount to any endeavor in which you find yourself charged is ensuring the development in consciousness of all concerned.

This objective often carries with it an extreme level of subjectivity. It is not, "What should be done to assist this individual?" but rather, "What needs to be done for the benefit of the Whole?" There will indeed be occasion when this decision is yours alone to resolve. Throughout the history of our work, real mistakes have been made by following the wrong course of action – mistakes that have ultimately been corrected or remain in the process of necessary amendment and rectification by the League.

Excerpt, "The Prime Directive," *A Time Traveler's Code of Conduct* **by Ruth #7**

TWO: *Journal Entry – April 3 ATL*

Although I shall henceforth be more attentive in such matters, it has been several weeks now since I have undertaken the opportunity to provide additional details as to the course of our activities during those first few days. My experience with the Kadesh situation was unlike anything I might have imagined, and it is only in the last day or two that I have even begun to feel like the younger version of my older self. Agnes #23 had, in fact, informed our class that these excursions into any timeline would take an energetic toll upon personal consciousness but hearing a fact and enduring it for oneself can be very different experiences indeed.

In the end, the discussion of Kadesh and its multiple timelines became only one of five "real-world examples" that Agnes chose for class examination throughout the days that followed. Agnes explained that these "mission assignments" were assigned to Wayfarers and students alike by the ATL Mission Office based upon a time traveler's individual background. On day number two, we explored the various timelines for a man named "Gates" and how a timeline with a focus on philanthropy was unquestionably a far better outcome than one bending toward global domination, or another related to the proclivities of a libertine, or a fourth in which he taught something called "computer science" at Harvard. Having ascertained the method by which these undertakings were dispersed, it came as no surprise to learn that the desired Gates' timeline directed toward philanthropic efforts became the very one assigned to my roomie George.

Undoubtedly, you may have already surmised that each of the three additional "real-world examples" was appropriately apportioned to my remaining classmates. Manuela #64 became the necessary inspiration for a man named "Chavez" and his efforts championing the rights of laborers. Bonne Soeur Marie #304 assisted a woman named "Nightingale" in choosing the path of a healer rather than one in which she became wedded to a British politician. The fifth timeline adjustment became coursework for Emanuel, who found himself as something of a spiritual liberator for the Roman named Saul.

To be sure, it was the Saul situation that gave me cause to wonder aloud whether Agnes (or the ATL Mission Office itself) was simply passing out timeline assignments that had already been rectified within the ATL parameters but our instructor refused to concede that these five were anything less than "absolutely necessary." Still, I remained somewhat convinced that these situations were more akin to "apprentice Wayfarer training" than to anything bordering on the real work of a journeyman time traveler. I even voiced these suspicions to George, who chose to remind me:

"Remember the solitary dot."

Nonetheless, I have vowed to keep track of the various timelines we encounter within the curriculum as a means of questioning additional recruits (when and if the opportunity ever presents itself) as to whether they themselves have had to deal with the very same classroom assignments.

In spite of much personal contemplation during those first days, I had yet to discern any appropriate course of action in the matter of the Ruth situation. I did not want to push the issue too forcefully with Agnes, as I had already inquired whether we might have the opportunity to be in the company of our personal recruiters. Our teacher seems to possess much personal clarity as to the exact enfoldment of the scheduled curriculum under her tutelage, and too many questions beyond the scope of the day's instruction have been repeatedly discouraged. Certainly, I dare not divulge to anyone the existence of what appears to be the hastily engraved lettering within my Horologium ("Help!R7") as the specificity of just whom or what Ruth #7 needs help with or from remains completely unknown to me.

Nevertheless, I have found a number of the lessons presented by Agnes #23 to be keenly fascinating as they explore topics I have yet to consider and often draw upon a seemingly boundless source of case illustrations. It did come as quite a surprise to learn that a number of individuals "crippled by the Collective Illusion" (I use this phrase as that is how Agnes chooses to describe it) were somehow able to perceive beyond the misperception of linear time. It may be edifying to detail at least one of her most recent examples:

According to Agnes, this narrative occurred "within the linear-timeline-perception of the twentieth century." Two women educators were on an excursion to Versailles. (I could report having been there myself but that account is entirely unnecessary to this tale.) At some point in the journey, they left behind other members of the tour and wandered off toward the Petit Trianon – a small chateau upon the grounds some distance away. As they traversed their chosen path, the two encountered numerous individuals garbed in attire that appeared to be from no less than 100 years previous. Arriving at the chateau, they found themselves in the presence of none other than Marie Antoinette and her entourage. Obviously frightened, the shock of encountering a long-dead queen caused the women to quickly retrace their steps. However, curiosity soon got the best of them and the two vowed to return, only to find that the pathway they had traveled existed no more. Finding another way, they arrived at the chateau but everything had changed, and the past with which they had just borne witness was gone. Once again, they were trapped within the confines of the Collective Illusion of their personal timeline. Worried that their contemporaries would surmise them to be of unsound mind, they chose a nom de plume and detailed their entire experience in a booklet. Apparently, that volume became popular in France when an eighteenth-century map specifically verified the pathway they had described in exact detail – a pathway that was evident no longer.

"That is the Moberly-Jourdain time slip!" Agnes

penned the name on the board, underlining the phrase twice over.

Certainly, this tale and others like it not only prompted personal fascination and the desire for additional examination but also the anticipation of firsthand study. It was this yearning for personal inspection, no doubt, that led me off in the direction of Kadesh with only some measure of trepidation – an account I will describe shortly.

Prior to the Kadesh excursion, I did find occasion to ask one question in regard to the young woman named Ruth, and its answer provided me with some small semblance of additional information during the end of that first week. One morning as she began her presentation, Agnes excitedly proclaimed to the class (stylus waving enthusiastically in the air before us) that there would be "some Core introductions" at the end of the day in which we would have a special opportunity to actually meet Sara #11 ("and a few others"). I should note that the phrase "a few others" was voiced with much less enthusiasm than the fanfare which had preceded it as the name "Sara #11!" was spoken aloud. It was those introductions at day's end that provided me with the very opportunity I had sought.

Near to the end of our class, an extremely attractive young woman came to the doorway with three others in close attendance. All at once Agnes #23 threw her hands in the air and exclaimed with joyful exuberance, "Oh, Sara, you have arrived!" Although Miss Sara did manage a smile in return, it seemed quite clear to any watchful observer that the enthusiasm displayed by our instructor was at least threefold that of the younger woman: "I am so glad you are able to visit!"

Agnes turned to the class and made it quite clear, *"This is a very special treat for you!"* She extended a greeting to each of the others while ushering them one by one into the room. As the group entered, I was immediately reminded of something Ruth had proclaimed not too many days previous within the confines of my own bedchamber: "We manage our appearance." The four newcomers had apparently chosen to "manage" how they presented themselves in varying degrees of seeming experience and personal maturity. Agnes #23 took the liberty of introducing them, one after the other.

"It is my pleasure to introduce Sara #11, our BELOVED Governor-General," Agnes gushed with absolute delight. "Sara oversees the entire workings of the League!"

Sara was quick to interrupt, "Along with the remaining Core," she added modestly.

"Absolutely," Agnes interjected, although it was quite clear that Agnes would have affirmed any words coming from the younger woman's mouth.

"This is Grimwald #94, a member of the Core and our Elder professor. He is responsible for overseeing the entire curriculum we have here at our school." Agnes nodded with approval.

Grimwald was a kindly-faced Black man, who possessed a healthy abundance of graying hair. As the eldest of our four visitors, his visage satisfied that of either an experienced educator or a senior pensioner. I presumed his chosen profession gave him at least some supervisory oversight regarding our teacher.

Next came, "This is Emma #119," a matronly woman who wore thin, black-rimmed spectacles, causing her to appear most stern in her stance. "In addition to being on the Core, she personally evaluates every single recruit recommendation that is submitted to the League." Agnes turned to the class and eyed her charges closely, "If it had not been for her final approval none of you would be here today."

Finally, "This is Milton #71. As a member of the Core, he manages the ATL Mission Office." Agnes nodded approvingly before continuing, "When you complete your time here in my class and have achieved the rank of journeyman Wayfarer, he will supervise each and every one of your mission assignments."

Milton wore the fine clothes of an English gentleman and his accent when speaking the words, "Happy to be in your presence," only confirmed my suspicions as to his country of origin.

Agnes made it clear that we had time for "just a few questions" before these members of the Core had to concern themselves with other matters of Core business. Manuela #64 went first, "How long has there been a League?"

The four visitors looked amongst themselves as though deciding who might best respond to the query until Sara #11 made the reply, "To ask 'how long' suggests there is a linear answer to this question, and I can only propose that this is not the case. It would be correct, however, to suggest that the League was present even at the instant Moment One first entered the Collective Illusion."

It was my merchant-banker-philanthropist-roomie who posed, "May I inquire as to how long you each have been members of the League?" (I made a mental note to myself to discuss with George the fact that anything to do with counting or ciphering or linear time would most probably not be a part of our present curriculum.)

"Another linear question," Emma sighed with some manner of impatience. "Suffice it to say that each of us has been involved in the League since long before the illusion of your most recent conception."

I decided it would not be inappropriate to voice

my own query, "Are there other members of the Core beyond you four before us?"

"There are," were the only words with which Emma chose to respond.

"Qui sont-ils? Who are they?" Bonne Soeur Marie asked before I had even been given the opportunity.

The question did not seem that difficult but the visitors glanced amongst themselves as though searching for the best possible response. Grimwald turned toward Sara, and I perceived some manner of general agreement between the two before he finally spoke, "Our numbers have changed at various stages of our work. At present, I believe there are 8 or 9 active members of the Core. That said, we rarely find either the occasion or the necessity of coming together as a whole."

"We have certainly benefited from the classroom text," I volunteered matter-of-factly. "May I inquire as to whether the author of the book, Ruth #7, is the very same individual who had occasion to serve as my personal recruiter?" The question seemed innocent enough.

Grimwald answered immediately, "It is." For a moment, he appeared to ponder providing an additional response but in the end he did not.

I continued my query, "Is Ruth #7 a member of the Core?"

At that very moment, Milton #71 chose to step forward and advise the class, "We must attend to other matters, but we four do wish to extend our hearty congratulations to each of you for the excellent work you displayed on your first mission assignments. Well done!"

Sara added, "And we must recognize Agnes #23 for her tremendous classroom instruction, making these achievements possible."

As I pondered the significance of there being no answer to my question about Ruth, Agnes blushed at the compliment she had received, and Emanuel spoke what I could only assume each of my classmates was thinking, "But we have yet to involve ourselves in any of these missions! Our assignments have been scheduled for later next week."

Sara smiled knowingly, "You are still thinking linear time. We have already availed ourselves of the Akasha and have witnessed the positive outcomes for which each and every one of you will be responsible. Milton is correct, we commend your endeavors." Sara then turned directly towards me, "We were extremely impressed with your ultimate course of action #239! Well done!"

Milton added, "Yes, Chap, that was a brilliant use of diplomacy!"

Before anything more could be said, the four turned and left the confines of the room.

As we each readied for our departures and the fulfillment of our respective mission assignments, I found myself exceedingly hopeful that whatever conclusion had caused Sara to call my first effort "well done" and Milton to compliment the work as "brilliant" would come easily to mind when the time came. I will only admit here to some measure of nervousness but certainly not the same level of apprehension that Agnes #23 appeared to be demonstrating in front of her entire class.

"Things will work out just fine. Things will work

out just fine." She anxiously moved about each of her students, stating the phrase repeatedly, perchance in an effort to calm herself. "We have thoroughly prepared for these assignments. We all know what we are doing!"

To be sure, we had all read and reread the process described by Ruth #7 in the textbook, and Agnes had frequently expounded upon the appropriate use of the Horologium: "1) Turn the hands of the watch clockwise for future events and counterclockwise for past events; 2) Give some measure of thought to the situation with which you are concerned; 3) Repeatedly say the name of the individual over which you hope to have some measure of influence; 4) Press the small button on the watch labeled 'TEMPUS' once; and, 5) Take a deep breath and relax."

I should note herein that a return trip to one's point of origin was accomplished by simply pressing the "TEMPUS" button three times over. Pressing said button twice allowed the traveler to revisit whatever mission one held in mind for possible correction or reset without encountering the previous version of one's own self who had made the selfsame journey.

After perceiving firsthand the difficulty with which Agnes #23 was able to control her unease, I could not help but wonder whether step number five was truly connected to the workings of the Horologium timepiece or had been added by our instructor as a means of calming herself. In either event, I did "take a deep breath and relax" immediately after pressing the "TEMPUS" button.

It may prove helpful to describe the events which followed from both my viewpoint as time traveler as well as the perspective of the targeted timeline recipient. At the outset, let me begin with my experience as a traveler.

Perhaps there have been occasions in which you

suddenly found yourself in a dream whereby you were falling without any control over said occurrence. For myself, when that transpires I become aware of the wind rushing past my extremities as my body plunges toward the ground below. It can be in no small measure a most frightening sensation, and the fright causes one's heartbeat to quicken seemingly out of control. I have come to believe that it is the beating of the heart that prompts one to awaken from such a dream.

Now imagine that selfsame experience in which you are falling but the sensation of falling goes on, and on, and on without interruption, and the swiftness of your heartbeat has no bearing whatsoever upon bringing the happening to a close. The sensation of falling continues, the swiftness of the heart goes on seemingly without end, and you find yourself incapable of being freed from the descent. In fact, the fall reaches its conclusion only with your arrival at the intended destination. If you can grasp some semblance of what bearing this would have upon you, then you will have some insight into the journey of a Wayfarer.

Since that first timeline mission, I have come to experience firsthand that the further one travels in this illusion of time in either direction (be it forward or backward), the longer one must undergo this process of descent. As my initial journey exceeded the span of three millennia, you might imagine that the fall was exceedingly long in duration. According to Agnes (as well as chapter four in the classroom text), this very process and the necessity of a return trip cannot help but take its toll upon every aspect of one's personal wellbeing. Such is the experience of a traveler.

It is perhaps best to assert from the very first that this mission of time traveling entails the movement of one's consciousness, not the physical body. It is only the mind that makes the journey. Our class text does indicate that the traveler is able to perceive the shadowy form of oneself but the book makes it extremely clear that one is not seeing the actual physical body. As to where the physical self may go, that remains completely unclear to me. It is certainly not explained by Ruth #7 in the text, and when Manuela #64 queried Agnes regarding that very subject our teacher's only response was, "Why does that matter?" Truly, I cannot say with certainty as to whether Agnes #23 did not know the answer, did not care about the answer, or did not wish to respond with an answer.

Having had the experience of witnessing the second mission of my roomie, George, ten days after our first assignments, I am able to describe here what I saw and heard firsthand. George stood at the front of the class, appearing very much prepared for the task. His manner was exceedingly calm and he nodded in my direction as to affirm his overall wellbeing. In spite of the fact that each of us had already completed a successful mission, Agnes continued to move about nervously, "You have prepared for this assignment. You know what you are doing! You know what you are doing?"

I watched as George turned the hands of his timepiece and closed his eyes, giving thought to the situation. After a moment, he began repeating the name, "Carnegie . . . Carnegie . . . Carnegie." His finger moved to push the "TEMPUS" button, and he took a breath. In the next instant, he was gone. His entire form disappeared from our view. It would be two days before he returned to the very same point, appearing very much the same as at the moment of his departure.

As to the whereabouts of his body in the interim, I do not know. Since that occasion, I have begun to ponder whether or not the physical body I once possessed (which was left in the charge of my grandsons to bury) is in fact gone, and the act of us "seeing" one another and oneself with physical forms may simply be a symptom of our own illusory making. Perhaps consciousness is all that exists, and all else is simply a perceived experience. However, I am not ready to conclusively make that argument, and I am certainly not of the opinion that Agnes #23 has any desire to discuss the matter as part of her classroom curriculum.

Let us now consider the selfsame event regarding my journey to Kadesh from the perspective of Ramesses, the timeline target. From the very first, it should be made exceedingly clear that Ramesses never truly became aware of my arrival or possessed incontrovertible evidence as to my presence. Having gone through the encounter myself, it has become quite clear as to how the intended recipient perceives the occurrence. If you have personally witnessed the passage of at least four decades, what I am about to describe will sound quite commonplace. In fact, the longer the extent of your life, the more familiarity you may have had with said experience.

Have you ever walked into a room and upon your arrival reflected for some measure of time as to the reason for entering that room in the first place? One moment the task you held in mind was perfectly clear and in the next instant you find that it is entirely gone. It is as if a fragment of your mind has completely disappeared. As a means of capturing the thought that is no longer present, you may even find yourself retracing the steps you took from your initial point of origin. That minuscule moment of complete forgetfulness is the very experience of the time traveler's recipient. It was this very impression that came to the mind of Ramesses as I took occasion to enter therein. The thought he had held in mind was suddenly no longer present.

To be sure, I am not suggesting that every time you walk into a room and forget why you made the journey to begin with, you may blame the activity of a time traveler but the truth of the matter is that if and when you do become a time traveler's intended target this will indeed be what you encounter. I have come to understand that the presence of these time travelers is much more commonplace than previously considered. After all, the League concerns itself with the consciousness of every individual in the whole world within every time period, therefore the numbers involved in this effort are most certainly numerous.

In any event, let me continue to depict my encounter with Ramesses. Although the text had covered the general experience with which one engages on these assignments, I came to discover that reading about the experience might best be described as an activity of the mind whereas the actual situation itself involves one's entire being. Upon my arrival at the intended destination, I became immediately aware that Ramesses was angry. He was angry that he had been cut off from three of his fighting divisions. He was angry at Muwatalli, the Hittite king. Angry that Muwatalli had continued these incursions into the Egyptian territory. Angry that Muwatalli did not respect the status of Pharaoh. He was intensely angry, and I could truly feel that anger.

Ramesses was in his preparation tent giving thought as to what would come next. He had already led the charge of his one remaining division and had chased the Hittite army to the edge of the river just outside the city of Kadesh. He was deciding whether to attack these forces and push them across the river's border, or continue to the city of Kadesh, or return to Egypt for reinforcements and attack the Hittite stronghold itself. As he pondered these various matters, it became clear that the Pharaoh's mind was uncertain as to his best course of action. Although pushing the Hittites across the river was within reach, if some portion of Muwatalli's forces were waiting for the opportunity to attack, without his remaining divisions he would be vulnerable. Any mistake on the part of the Pharaoh could result in his own death as well as the death of his men. Doubt had entered his mind.

While aware of all that transpired within the deliberations of Ramesses, I became cognizant of my own thoughts. I became aware of the smells of perfume that an Egyptian attendant seemed eager to distribute throughout the enclosure. The scents reminded me of cinnamon, frankincense, and flowers in the springtime. I became conscious of the fact that through the Pharaoh himself I could see, hear, smell, and feel the touch of my surroundings. When I gave thought to these observations, I made a mental note that in the next mission I should find occasion to "taste" something, as well.

While all this transpired, I perceived my own ghostly form walking in step with the Pharaoh. It was clear that my vaporous self was not evident to Ramesses but I was there, still clutching the shadowy form of the Horologium in my palm. I chose to extend my other hand as far away from the Pharaoh as possible to see if it could be done. It did move quite some distance apart from the bronze coat he wore, yet I still found myself possessing some measure of attachment to his every movement and thought.

I will disclose here that prior to my mission descent, I had some unease as to whether or not I would truly have the capacity to understand Ramesses' thoughts, let alone the Egyptian language, but the experience was very different than thinking words or understanding a native tongue. Yes, I seemed to understand Ramesses (both his thoughts and his speech) but I can only describe it as being very different than dealing with specific words. Although obviously feeble in comparison, I might describe the activity as being somewhat akin to going for a walk or finding occasion to take a swim. Both of these activities involve one's whole self but at no point does one have to think, "I must put this foot in front of the other" or "I must reach out with my left hand in the water and pull back toward myself as I reach out with my right." One just experiences the walk or the swim – the process is not something to which self must give thought. That was my experience within the consciousness of Ramesses. I was very much aware of all that transpired around me but it was not something I needed to give mind to in an effort to understand.

Perhaps this should have been mentioned earlier for clarity but I will interject it now. The greatest limitation facing a Wayfarer is that a time traveler cannot impose an idea upon the mind of his or her intended target unless that idea is already somewhere present within the individual. In other words, I could not convince the Pharaoh to undertake some possibility that did not already exist within his own mind. From the viewpoint of Ramesses's consciousness, it was exceedingly clear that his primary desire was to win against the Hittite king. He had to win, just as his own father before him, Seti, would have won. He had to be the victor. This was the state of mind I encountered.

One of the primary objectives of any good diplomat is to find common ground upon which all parties might agree. Since I now knew the mind of Ramesses, it was therefore time to explore the very consciousness of the

Hittite King, Muwatalli.

I allowed my ghostly form to touch the hands of the Horologium and rather than moving the time mechanism to the left or to the right, I gave it a gentle tap with my forefinger as my desire was to remain within the time period in which I now found myself. I gave thought to the situation, repeatedly said the name "Muwatalli," pushed the "TEMPUS" button, took a breath, and I was off.

I would not so much describe what came next as a fall or a descent but rather more akin to a leap. One moment I was with Ramesses, and then it felt as if I took a leap and found myself in the mind of Muwatalli, and Muwatalli was mad. He was mad at Ramesses, this child of a Pharaoh who gave much greater thought to his own importance than was either called for or deserved. He was mad at Seti, the father of Ramesses, who had been the one responsible for taking the city of Kadesh from the Hittites in the first place. He was angry that Ramesses did not respect his position as king of the Hittite nation. He was mad, and he wanted nothing more than to win in a battle against the Egyptian. He had to win. He had to win to recapture the honor that had been lost with the fall of Kadesh.

As I felt these thoughts come to me, I suddenly understood that Muwatalli's forces exceeded those of Ramesses by more than two to one. Muwatalli would easily prove the victor. At the same time, however, the thought gave way to a concern held within the mind of the Hittite king himself that although he would win this day against Ramesses, whatever Pharaoh came next would have no choice but to attack the Hittites as a means of upholding Egyptian honor. Muwatalli was well aware that the entirety of forces within the Egyptian empire far exceeded his own. Although he would win the battle of Kadesh, his victory would inevitably lead to his own destruction. Still, he had no choice but to win.

I must admit the solution came to me much more swiftly than I might have imagined. It was exceedingly clear that all things must have their place. I could not simply let the Egyptians win, nor could I try to achieve a conquest solely for the Hittites. Ramesses had to win in the same way that Muwatalli had to win. The solution was simple – both sides would claim victory. Ramesses would claim triumph because he had moved the Hittite division to the border of the river. Muwatalli's claim of victory would be due to the fact that he could have used his forces to eliminate both Pharaoh and the Egyptian army and had not.

Once the diplomatic solution was at hand, it was a relatively simple proposition to switch back and forth between either ruler, giving voice to each, their individual proclamation of victory, and the desired truce for a peaceful end to the conflict. The Hittite king dispatched a messenger toward the Egyptian army suggesting just such an outcome. A moment later, Ramesses dispatched his own messenger with virtually the selfsame approach. A simple announcement of victory and peace seemed sufficient for either side – the actual treaty would be drawn on a later occasion.

The days that followed were filled with little more than fatigue. Time travel does take its toll upon one's personal fortitude. It proved to be not just my experience but the experience of each of my classmates, as well. Agnes #23 explained that as we were new to this process, there would be a "one-time exception" to our normal course of instruction. Thankfully, no classes were scheduled for several days following our first mission assignments.

Our instructress also took occasion to make it quite clear that after a mission each of us would be required to discuss our experiences as part of our "classwork participation grade." In spite of her declaration, George and I took the liberty of describing our respective experiences prior to the class review. I was just as eager to hear details of George's involvement with the "Gates" situation as I was to tell him of my own. I must admit that George's reflection required a great deal further elucidation in the matter of "computers," and "software," and "electronic communication," and "Microsoft," and so forth, whereas my own details regarding Ramesses and the Hittites seemed much more straightforward by comparison.

It was a relief to find that I had almost completely regained my strength and composure by the time class instruction resumed. After that first mission involving the Egyptian Pharaoh himself, however, imagine my surprise when Agnes #23 informed me that my second assignment was to involve none other than His Imperial Majesty, the British King.

Although slight variations in history may be capable of maintaining the overall sanctity of a timeline and the Collective Illusion which results, the Core has found occasion when even the smallest change can engender major disruptions in the Akasha.

While all events out of harmony with the ATL must eventually be rectified by members of the League, there is ever the potential that this process can create enormous delays in our ultimate destiny. To be sure, the tragedy this brings into manifestation becomes nothing less than the elongation of space-time itself, and a postponement of that Consciousness which existed prior to Moment One.
   Excerpt, "Revisiting Your Timeline Assignment," *A Time Traveler's Code of Conduct* **by Ruth #7**

THREE: *Journal Entry – April 9 ATL*

What may be of greatest interest concerning the days which followed was perhaps the activity of being able to pursue all manner of information and knowledge, as well as my encounters with two very different kings. The most notable experience in the first regard began with Agnes #23 bobbing about as she wrote two words "FIELD TRIP" on the board while stating with more enthusiasm and fanfare than seemed necessary, "Today we will have our field trip!" It was only shortly thereafter that I came to the full realization our scheduled curriculum for the day had absolutely nothing to do with a "field" nor did said "trip" entail actually leaving the facility.

It soon became exceedingly clear that the League building was far larger than anything I might have ever imagined. Agnes led the five of us through one hallway after another, chattering to herself with a continual series of declarations, "You are all going to be amazed," and "I can still remember my very first visit," and "This is the place that makes our work truly possible!" We followed her down one corridor, and then another hallway, all the while making enough unfamiliar turns for it to become quickly evident that I would require either written directions or some semblance of a map if the need arose for a return trip. It was only after George and I had glanced at one another several times over as though to inquire of the other, "How much longer?" that we finally found ourselves standing before an enormous double doorway. Upon one of the doors had been placed a handwritten sign: "Akasha temporarily closed for new student orientation." Agnes #23 flung open the other doorway and ushered us all inside an immense library. To be sure, the chamber was larger than anything I had ever seen before.

There were books as far as any of us could see – thousands of books, hundreds of thousands, millions. The volumes were neatly organized on countless shelves that rose several stories above the ground. Agnes led us towards a large open space that seemed to serve as some manner of central antechamber or reception hall, as the stacks of books fanned out from this point in many directions. We walked toward an elderly bearded man, dressed in white, who stood at the very center of the chamber. As I looked upon his bearded countenance, I imagined that should the need ever arise for me to imagine the visage of the Maker of the Universe such might appear very much akin to the old man standing before us.

Agnes seemed full of pride as she pointed toward the elderly gentleman and informed us, "This is Emmett.

He is in charge of these records and knows absolutely everything. Just absolutely everything!"

The old man seemed appreciative of the introduction, acknowledged our teacher, and then turned toward us. "Welcome to the Akasha." Although definitely old, he did not appear in any way troubled by movement or gait or afflicted with (as I would come to discover) impediment of thought.

Agnes introduced the five of us to Emmett, who nodded and replied, "I am familiar with each of you."

"I told you, he knows absolutely everything," Agnes repeated excitedly, "absolutely everything!"

My roomie sighed aloud with utter amazement, "I have never before seen such an enormous library! This is incredible!"

Emmett concurred, "This is only the central facility. We have many, many specialized collections beyond the central chamber."

"Where do all the passages lead?" Manuela #64 pointed in the direction of one of the enormous corridors of books. On either side of each passageway, the shelves continued for immense distances, even beyond where we stood.

Emmett pointed toward the signage that lined each end of the book stacks facing us. "Every passageway and corridor is marked and each contains specific information that a Wayfarer may need in the performance of her or his duties. In this direction, you will find 'things that might have been.'" He pointed toward his left. Next, he pointed in back of us, "Behind you, you will find 'things as they currently are.'" He motioned over his shoulders behind himself, "Here you will discover 'things that may still be.'" Finally, he pointed to his right, "These are the 'things that should be.'"

"The ATL – Approved Timeline," Agnes said aloud.

"Exactly," came Emmett's confirmation. "Obviously, due to the nature of our collection, there is some overlap of information within these various categories."

Soeur Marie appeared totally spellbound by our surroundings and after glancing in every direction as though in search of something exclaimed aloud, "C'est merveilleux . . . It is wonderful! Surely you are not the only one attending to all these books. Where are the others?"

Emmett replied, "There is only me. I am the Keeper of the Records."

Agnes could not contain her excitement, "Emmett and Miss Sara have been a part of the League from the very first, and Emmett has been a part of the library ever since. You cannot imagine the number of questions he receives, and his patience is never-ending! He knows absolutely everything!"

The old man simply responded, "As long as there has been the Akasha, I have been here. Sara #11 and I were the first recruits. Between us, we assembled the Core."

"Truly, it is incredible!" Emanuel #41 finally managed to say. "I have never seen a place such as this before!"

Emmett nodded, "It is a wonder. There are volumes for every thought, every possibility, every individual."

I chose to add my own reflection to the discussion, "Does this operate as a lending library of some manner?"

"The books are never taken from the collection. To view these materials requires one's presence."

I continued, "And who has access to the collection?"

"League students, Wayfarers, members of the Core." Emmett added, "Over time, there have also been a number of individuals who – in spite of their attachment to the Collective Illusion – have managed to discover our facility. No one who arrives at the Akasha library is denied access."

"Are you saying there are *those still alive* who have somehow found their way to the library?" Emanuel queried.

"To be sure . . . clairvoyants, spiritual adepts, and the like," the old man stated matter-of-factly. "However, I assure you, only their consciousness has made the journey."

"Are volumes ever added to the collection?" came my final question.

Emmett appeared to sigh when he said, "Yes, with great regularity but thankfully much of the collection is automated."

When we had all taken the opportunity to voice our queries, Agnes announced, "Emmett will guide us all through the facility. Afterward, during your 'free time,' I would encourage you to find information that will help you fulfill your next mission assignments." She paused momentarily as she pulled a folded piece of paper from her dress pocket, "I brought a list." She unfolded the paper and read aloud:

"Manuela #64, you will want to explore the issue of child labor between 1880 and 1938, as well as the records of both Lewis Hine and Edgar Gardner Murphy."

Agnes turned next to Emanuel, "Look into the life experience of both John Wesley and George Whitefield, and discover whatever you can about their influence and rivalry regarding the Methodist revival movement."

Moving to Bonne Soeur Marie, Agnes suggested, "It could be very advantageous for you to familiarize yourself with the first school of medicine – Greek history, fourth century, before current illusion."

My roomie was next, "George #111, I would recommend a 'background mission,' looking into Islam's pillar of faith known as the Zakat, the giving of alms to the poor."

Finally, it was my turn, "Ben #239, you might want to explore the topic of British royalty in the lead-up to World War II."

George turned to me in horror, "There was a world war?"

"It would appear that there have been at least two," was all I managed to say.

After obtaining a copy of the "officially approved League student handout" from Agnes which illustrated the return trip to the Akasha, I was able to undertake two full afternoons of personal inquiry. The repeated assistance of Emmett was invaluable, as he frequently directed me toward the correct passageway or somehow managed to appear at just the right moment (often clutching the very volume I needed for additional research). In the end, it became very clear that the myth of the man who would become king was very different than the man himself. To be sure, Edward, Prince of Wales, was an enigma. Raised in the royal household, he loved every freedom that was afforded him but loathed any obligation that came as a result. He was strong-willed, determined, and obstinate in all things save his relationships with women in which he was weak, subservient, and unsteady. A chance meeting at a party had prompted him to essentially trade one married mistress for another, replacing Thelma Furness (who had replaced Freda Ward before her) with Wallis Simpson.

Having frequently succumbed to the passions of youth myself, I could certainly understand falling under the influence of a good woman but the prince seemed ever drawn to one inappropriate relationship after another. To be sure, his weakness with women was not his sole deficiency. The evidence I encountered suggested that he loved money above duty, title above honor, and privilege above equality.

"He will become King?" I looked up from the stack of books in front of me.

The old man nodded in the affirmative, "Upon the death of his father, King George V on January 20, 1936, he will become Edward VIII."

I pointed to the research materials upon the desk and voiced that which seemed all too clear, "It appears that which would follow remains somewhat uncertain."

"You are correct. Although the ATL would have him abdicate on December 11, 1936, that is only one of several possible outcomes."

"Do any of these possibilities possess more certainty than others?"

Emmett nodded, "To be sure. There are two that remain equal to the ATL. In timeline XXV, Edward marries Wallis Simpson, chooses not to abdicate, and as a means of bargaining with Parliament proposes that Wallis not receive the title of queen and that his brother's children become next in line as heirs to the throne."

"And the problem?"

"The couple will align with Germany, choosing neutrality and nonintervention as Hitler marches west . . . You have seen some of the information on Hitler, no doubt?"

"Yes," came my only reply.

"The other is timeline LII, in which Edward does not meet Wallis Simpson until after his coronation. Instead, once assuming the throne, he marries his mistress, Thelma Furness. Under her influence and her desire to become queen, he refuses to abdicate, and the act leads to a constitutional crisis in Parliament for more than two years – a crisis which leaves England ill-prepared for war. In the midst of such chaos, Winston Churchill fails in his attempt to become Prime Minister."

"It would appear that Edward must choose Wallis Simpson and he must choose to abdicate the throne."

"That is the approved timeline."

Once my investigation had been completed and I had reviewed the process of travel with Agnes #23 yet again (in spite of my repeated protests that I had already become extremely familiar with the procedure), it was not long thereafter that I found myself literally within the very presence of Edward, Prince of Wales himself. A turn of the Horologium's hands to the left, sufficient contemplation upon the matter, the twofold repetition of an absurdly long name ("Edward Albert Christian George Andrew Patrick David Windsor"), a press of the "TEMPUS" button, along with a breath of air, followed by a much shorter descent than my first outing, and I soon found myself within the mind of a prince. And it was the prince who sat stubbornly on the other side of an enormous desk, across from his father, George V, King of the United Kingdom, and Emperor of India.

"It is entirely inappropriate," the king coughed several times while managing to take an exceedingly long breath through his cigarette, ". . . inappropriate that my son and heir to the British throne should continue in these illicit liaisons with married and divorced women. It must stop!" The outburst caused him to cough anew.

As the king spoke, I could feel both frustration and irritation pass through Edward's entire body. Edward seemed to consider his father both a nuisance and an impediment to his life. At least for the moment to which I bore witness, the thoughts of the Prince of Wales appeared devoid of any affection toward the man.

King George coughed, inhaled deeply from his cigarette, coughed again, and added, "I continue to find myself entirely disappointed in this inability of yours to settle down. You need to find a wife who is fit to become queen ... do you understand?" When there came no response, the king added, "It is your duty to the Empire!"

Edward was furious. He chose not to express most of the things I could see passing through his mind save one, "I did not choose to be king."

Between coughs, the king was quick to respond, "Nor did I, but it is the burden that has been thrust upon us. When will you cease in this foolishness?"

I could plainly see that Edward was quite near allowing the words, "bugger off" to fall from his lips but a quick change of thought (on his own part, I might add) prompted him to say instead, "Father, you cannot tell me who I may choose to spend my time with . . . these are friends. *They are my friends."*

The king shook his head in dismay, "I am not a fool. Do you not understand that everyone within these walls knows what you are up to? It has to stop!"

Edward moved to speak but said nothing. As the king placed the remnants of his cigarette in the ashtray in front of him, Edward shook his head in defiance.

The king lifted the cigarette package from his desk. Finding it empty, he crushed it within his hand and tossed it aside. At that moment, I looked upon my own transparent fingers (floating hazily within Edward's hand) and chose to use the Horologium to move my consciousness to that of the king instead. Just as I pressed the button and breathed, King George moved to speak but suddenly stopped. For an instant, he seemed to be recollecting his thoughts.

Once I became aware of my own presence within him, the king stared across the desk at his eldest son, Edward, where I had resided only a moment before. I could feel King George's thoughts becoming calmer, choosing instead a different manner of approach, "Your brother, Albert . . . Bertie was lucky enough to find Mary. Surely your luck can change but you must stop looking in the wrong place. Can you give it a try?"

Edward appeared to sigh with some measure of resignation before finally saying, "I can try, father, but I can only be myself."

The Prince of Wales rose and walked toward the doorway. He opened the door and seemed to acknowledge the presence of someone standing in the hallway before turning to tell his father, "The Prime Minister wishes to see you." Edward then turned and left.

"My dear Baldwin, please come in." The king rose for a moment and acknowledged Prime Minister Stanley Baldwin, motioning him toward the very chair in which Edward had just been sitting.

"How was the conversation, Your Majesty?"

Within the mind of the king, I could see that he and Baldwin had discussed the matter of Edward previously.

"Not good . . . not good at all." I sensed the king's thoughts turn to another cigarette, and he immediately opened a desk drawer, fumbling for a moment to find one. After opening the pack and taking one in hand, he lit it and took a long draw, "After I am dead, I fear that boy will ruin himself within twelve months." He coughed several times before adding, "I pray to God that Edward will never marry or have children and that nothing will ever come between Bertie, and Lilibet, and the throne."

With some semblance of personal knowledge and experience already in hand regarding the prince, I found it a simple matter really to turn the Horologium to the left and travel backward in time several years earlier. My intended target for the journey (which entailed more than a leap but truly not a major fall) was Thelma Furness, with whom Edward, Prince of Wales had been keeping time.

Within moments of my arrival I knew that Thelma loved her four-year-old son, William, immensely, but not very far behind was her love for both money and title, and Marmaduke Furness, her husband (whom she called "Duke") had both. He was First Viscount, making her Viscountess, and his shipping empire had made him extremely wealthy. It soon became clear in my mind, however, that Thelma had grown tired of him. In spite of the child between them, Duke continued to pine after his first wife, Daisy, who had died during a botched abdominal surgery. The Duke's grief had turned first to depression and then toward alcohol. When sober, he spoke only of ships and business; when bent, his limited conversation expanded to include Daisy. In Thelma's mind, she considered him a bore. She turned her thoughts to Prince Edward instead.

I could see the image of the prince moving about her head. She pictured the two of them together . . . together as husband and wife. I immediately sensed what had attracted Thelma Furness to the Prince of Wales in the first place. Setting aside her proclivity for men in general, she was captivated by his wit, his love of conversation, his willingness to follow her lead, and his ready pursuit of whatever celebration, party, or bash appeared next upon the calendar. The Duke's ongoing occupation with business, his travel schedule, and his propensity to binge for days on end had made an alliance with Edward quite easy to maneuver, and it was Edward upon whom she had next set her sights.

Edward had more money than God Himself, and a title that was three or four levels above that of her husband's. His penchant for lovemaking was also a far notch above her current situation. Truly, she was smitten with this prince who would become king. Yes, she would sue Duke for divorce, and marry Edward David Windsor. In time, she would become Queen Consort. Surely, that was a title fit for a woman of her standing.

With Thelma's final thought still in mind, I took hold of my Horologium and moved on.

The two half-days I had spent within the many corridors and passageways of the Akasha library had provided me with both clarity and insight. Rectifying the issue with timeline LII, and making certain that Edward did, in fact, meet Wallis Simpson certainly appeared to be within my capabilities. Viscountess Furness ("Thelma") had given a party at Burrough Court, her estate. For one reason or another Duke was indisposed for the occasion, providing Edward the opportunity to serve as her escort. Emmett had shown me the essential problem within timeline LII was simply that one couple had canceled at the last minute, and after pondering the matter for only a moment, Thelma had chosen not to replace them. It was this very act of not inviting another couple that had given rise to the issue of Edward and Wallis not meeting before the coronation. Certainly, it was easy enough to revisit that decision and instead invite another pair with whom Thelma was extremely familiar – after all, she and the wife had much in common. Both women were previously divorced and both were expatriate Americans. The husband was Ernest Simpson and his wife was named "Wallis." Truly, the irony was not lost on me that it would be Thelma herself who would undermine her own plans for the future, introducing Edward to the very woman who would come after.

Assuring that Wallis Simpson was invited to the party was straightforward enough. The issue was addressed relatively easily and soon rectified by the Horologium. I knew from the information I had obtained while visiting the Akasha that during the party Edward would become enthralled with Wallis Simpson, finding her absolutely "sympathetic, understanding, and witty." Their relationship would begin shortly thereafter. With the passage of time, Wallis would convince Edward to bring an end to all of his other dealings with married and divorced women. The two would become a couple, and the Prince of Wales would become king on January 20, 1936, upon the death of his father.

Certainly, these matters can be filled with any number of complications. For ease of understanding, I choose here only to elucidate upon the essential details providing clarity to the tale. According to the books that Emmett had gathered together for my research, the new king would soon grow extremely tired of duty, responsibility, and his never-ending schedule of royal audiences. In order to "rejuvenate himself," Edward VIII decided to take a Mediterranean cruise aboard the luxury yacht Nahlin, bringing with him none other than his married mistress, Wallis Simpson. The decision had been both dangerous and reckless, and soon became fodder for news stories throughout Europe and the States. This Mediterranean journey provided the king's subjects with unbecoming insights into his personal life. Many were enraged that he – as "Head of the Church of England!" – was spending time with a once divorced, still married woman; others were just as upset that this woman happened to be "an American!" The news and the public dismay would lead to a meeting between the king and the prime minister, and it was that very meeting I turned to next, setting my target upon the prime minister himself.

I found Prime Minister Baldwin sitting in the very chair he had often occupied in conversations with Edward's father. He leaned forward, straightened his gray waistcoat, and gathered his thoughts. The younger king was too stubborn for his own good and would not listen to reason. The prime minister tried yet again to express the seriousness of the situation:

"This has become a matter of State," Your Majesty. "It is no longer simply the purview of Your Majesty and Mrs. Simpson. "

Edward's irritation was evident, "Wallis and I plan to marry."

"She is divorced and still married to her second husband. This cannot be."

"I am king!" Edward was adamant. "I will marry the woman I love."

"The Archbishop of Canterbury has condemned the affair. He will not allow it."

Each of the words that came next were stated slowly,

as though the king were speaking to a child, "Then we shall find another Archbishop."

The thoughts that passed before me made it extremely clear that Baldwin had become tired of these discussions. Within the year he would be 70, and contemplating the freedom of retirement was now frequently entertained within his mind. The prospect of arguing on the king's behalf in front of the House of Commons was something that he absolutely disdained. Still, he wished to avoid a parliamentary crisis at all costs.

"What do you propose?" the prime minister inquired.

"I suggest a 'Morganic marriage.' I shall choose my brother as heir apparent and Wallis will renounce the royal title."

Baldwin shook his head in frustration, "I fear a constitutional crisis may be the result, and the Archbishop will never keep quiet in this matter. You need to reconsider this, Your Majesty. You need to seriously reconsider."

I could see Baldwin wondering to himself why the king was even taking such a stance, as Edward absolutely abhorred royal duties to begin with, preferring instead the company of a woman, the opportunity for leisure, and all manner of carefree pursuit. As this very thought passed through the prime minister's mind, I suddenly had an idea. The idea prompted a decision to revisit the same meeting, yet again.

My vaporous hand took hold of the time mechanism, and I gave thought to repeating the very conversation I had just witnessed. After reciting "Stanley Baldwin" several times over and pressing the button twice so as to avoid encountering my previous self, I took a deep breath, and a moment later found myself back where I had started not fifteen minutes before.

Let me begin by confirming one of the statements

contained within our classroom text. I remember reading Ruth's words, *"Once interaction with a timeline has occurred, space-time is altered ever so slightly."* As soon as I returned to the start of the meeting, I noticed there was indeed a change. Prime Minister Baldwin was wearing very different attire than he had worn previously. Rather than his gray waistcoat, Baldwin sat before the king in a black suit and tie. I glanced about the room as a means of identifying other changes, as well, and although papers upon the king's desk seemed somewhat different than they had appeared previously, I could not swear to it with any degree of certainty. Still, there was no doubt, he wore a different suit.

Baldwin repeated his very words from before: "This has become a matter of State, Your Majesty. "It is no longer simply the purview of Your Majesty and Mrs. Simpson. "

Edward was extremely irritated as he spoke, "Wallis and I plan to marry."

"She is divorced and still married to her second husband. This cannot be."

"I am king!" Edward was adamant. "I will marry the woman I love."

"The Archbishop of Canterbury has condemned the affair. He will not allow it."

"Then we shall find another Archbishop."

It was at that moment I took the opportunity and brought forth from the prime minister's own thoughts various reflections he had often wished to communicate, beginning with, "Your Majesty, you and I both know that you are not fond of these royal duties, and have little patience with matters of State. Surely, your time could be better spent in activities more pleasing to your nature and stature in life?"

The king inquired, "What do you propose?"

Although Baldwin spoke the words cautiously, the words were his own: "If you were to abdicate the throne in favor of your brother, you would have far greater freedom to marry as you choose . . . and, as you would no longer be Head of the Church, the Archbishop could hold no influence over the decision."

Baldwin paused for a moment to gauge the king's response. It seemed clear that His Majesty was listening, waiting for additional information.

"I would also suggest that it would not be at all inappropriate for your brother to pay you an annual allowance as former king."

King Edward VIII nodded at the idea with some measure of satisfaction.

Baldwin added for additional emphasis, "The allowance would be entirely sufficient to ensure your continued station and wellbeing."

After several moments of contemplation, Edward managed to say: "I believe that sounds acceptable."

Although it appeared evident that the mission had been a success, as a means of confirming all outstanding issues had been truly rectified within the ATL, I took the Horologium in hand and chose to move forward to the broadcast date of Edward VIII's abdication speech.

I experienced a slight fall, and then suddenly found myself as witness to December 11, 1936. I could see the ghostly form of my hands floating around the hands of the king himself as he held the typewritten pages. He read the words before him into the microphone, making it possible for British subjects the world over to hear everything he said: "I have found it impossible to carry the heavy burden of responsibility and to discharge my duties as king as I would wish to do without the help and support of the woman I love . . ."

At that point, I pushed "TEMPUS" three times,

although I must confess that while traversing the journey home I could not help but wonder what it might have been like to encounter a version of my previous self.

I had promised my roomie that I would immediately discuss all that had transpired upon my arrival but, unfortunately, at Emmett's insistence, I had told him the very same thing. It was for that reason that I found myself traveling the various hallways and turns that led back to the Akasha. Yes, I was tired, and it was true that I only wished to go back to my own chamber and rest but the satisfaction of completing another mission, coupled with the desirability of informing Emmett as to exactly what had transpired, provided me with sufficient vigor to make the journey. I was delighted that things had worked out. I also found myself extremely impressed with how accurately the Akasha had portrayed the very information I had seen firsthand. I could not help but wonder if there might be a way to use the library in my own quest to assist Ruth.

That solitary thought provided me with some measure of stamina to continue the rest of the way. I have to admit some semblance of amusement as I opened the double door and suddenly became cognizant of the fact that, as Keeper of the Akasha, Emmett could have already explored the records regarding my mission and all that had taken place. I walked toward the center of the chamber where Emmett stood waiting before me.

"I assume you know that I have completed the assignment?" I asked aloud.

Emmett looked around as if to confirm we were alone. "I am grateful you have returned," he said somberly. "I need to speak with you."

I could not help but feel some measure of frustration that he had failed to even acknowledge the mission he had asked to hear about; nonetheless, I inquired, "Regarding?"

"It is a matter of grave importance," he said mysteriously. "I believe I can trust you. I have thoroughly examined the records of your personal work. I need to tell you something."

"What is it?"

Emmett glanced about nervously and appeared extremely cautious as he spoke what followed: "Someone has altered the records. I do not know who is responsible but the official records have been modified. The approved timeline has been changed."

To control time and space can be the ultimate path of service, for it entails great personal sacrifice, the laying aside of selfish agendas, and a commitment to helping the Whole without thought of personal gain. Your induction into the League, however, is not without extreme personal temptation and, unfortunately, it is a temptation that every recruit must face in her or his own journey.

For to control time and space avails itself of the possibilities of great wealth and nearly limitless power but should you choose this path (as some have done before you), know that it is an illusory path of temporary pleasure, no more real than the Collective Illusion itself. Most importantly, once this path is chosen you are in direct opposition to the mission of the League and may find yourself subject to personal eradication by the Core.

Excerpt, "Choosing Darkness or Choosing Light," *A Time Traveler's Code of Conduct* **by Ruth #7**

FOUR: Journal Entry – April 11 ATL

I must admit that the matter of Emmett's allegation continued to weigh heavily upon my mind. Although Emmett had asked me to withhold discussing the matter as he wished to undertake further investigation, his admission only heightened my unease regarding the Ruth situation. I found myself questioning the legitimacy of virtually everyone around me. I am not given to fanciful conspiracies nor do I expect to find treachery lurking about every corridor but something appeared to be happening that was neither in the open nor a portion of the League's sanctioned activities. Repeatedly, I could not help but wonder who might be trusted. I had almost decided to report the entire situation to my roomie when it occurred to me that if someone was trying to mislead me, providing me with an associate like George would engender a most brilliant form of deception. To be sure, as quickly as the thought had entered my mind, I brushed it aside and assured myself that imagining such a scheme was falling prey to the very intrigue I abhorred. After ruminating upon the idea, I decided that even if and when I communicated my fears to George, he would be no more capable of addressing the situation than myself. For that reason, I assumed discussing the unusual matter of my Horologium ("Help!R7") with Emmett was arguably the best course of action. Whatever his incentive, the Keeper of the Records had chosen to take me into his confidence; I vowed to do the same.

Unfortunately, the rigor of our class curriculum and Agnes #23's ongoing oversight made such an opportunity somewhat evasive over the days which followed. On more than one occasion our instructor's presentation of the curriculum had challenged every measure of mental acuity that I might bring to the classroom. I found such to be the case when Agnes took stylus in hand and began her lesson with the statement, "Even physicists crippled by the Collective Illusion of the twenty-first century have discovered that the length of time between perceived events is somehow interwoven and dependent upon the observer."

Beginning with the word "physicist," which was totally unknown to me at the time, I regarded the rest of the statement which followed as seemingly beyond any semblance of personal comprehension. It was only later (while foregoing the hubbub of the League café and waiting instead within our chamber for the bell to announce the completion of mid-morning break) that George provided some clarity to my confusion by discussing his own take on the matter:

"I believe the statement suggests that the perception of time is connected to the individual's experience of it. I have given thought to an experience that may more readily illustrate just how often perception imbues one's personal situation."

"Go on," I motioned with my hand for him to continue.

"Think of it this way . . ." George collected his thoughts, causing me to become fairly certain that a tale fit for either a banker or a merchant was certain to follow. "While in London, I often found reason to distribute a half-a-crown to the needy and unfortunate. As you know, its value is two shillings and sixpence. On occasion when I placed that coin in a palm, it was as if I had given away the crown jewels themselves – there came tears of joy and expressions of unlimited gratitude, all due to a single half-a-crown." George smiled broadly as he called the memory to mind.

"However," George continued, "there were several instances when, as I turned loose of the coin, the recipient looked upon me with anger, and stated in no uncertain terms that I had it within my power to provide much more. In each case, the need was evident and the coin was the same, but the perceived value became very much qualified by the individual receiving it."

I grasped his analogy immediately, "I do understand! Had Agnes suggested instead that the passage of time of which I grew mindful while discussing matters of the day with my associates was far shorter in duration than that experienced by my wife Deborah as she waited at home for my return, I would have comprehended immediately. Surely, the influence of one's perception cannot be ignored in matters such as these."

At that very moment, the bell rang and I encouraged us both, "Let us sally forth."

I have never considered myself a particularly religious man, choosing instead to pursue the lifelong goal of moral perfection. That said, I am not averse to imploring the assistance of Heaven from time to time, or asking the Maker of the Universe for support in the success of occasional deliberations. I provide this information solely to demonstrate my openness to the matter of prayer, especially since the topic became the subject of one of the more unusual case histories Agnes chose for discourse later that day. Whether it was Agnes's description itself or simply the nature of the situation, I must confess some perplexity in being able to adequately relate an explanation of the story but, nonetheless, I provide my attempt herewith:

To begin, Agnes #23 used her stylus to write the name, "Dr. Leonard Leibovici" on the board as well as the words, "Rabin Medical Center." As was her preferred method of emphasis, she underscored both sets of terms twice over, and assured us this would be a further illustration of the fact that those "crippled by the Collective Illusion of time" had the opportunity to see beyond the fallacy of their misperceptions, "If only they would choose to look!"

For the hour which ensued, we were provided with (what Agnes chose to call) "sufficient background information" as a means of understanding the narrative, including the fact that within the approved timeline of the twentieth century there arose a Jewish nation called "Israel." Apparently, it is a small country on the eastern shore of the Mediterranean Sea, and in such a place came to be a city called "Tel Aviv." It was near this city one could find the Medical Center as well as Dr. Leonard in particular, who resides at the very heart of the tale. We also learned of something called a "bloodstream infection," which is part of the story, and how said infection can lead to fever, further illness, and even death. When Agnes determined that the background she had provided was wholly sufficient, she proceeded to inform us that, "On the surface, Dr. Leonard's research appears to deal with the subject of prayer but it is about much, much more!"

Let me interject that with mention of the word "prayer," our French lass Bonne Soeur Marie #304 found cause to sit up with rapt attention. Suddenly, she possessed more enthusiasm than at any other time I had witnessed, save for the possible exception of her relating the "Florence Nightingale mission" after its completion. Soeur Marie excitedly informed us that the subject of prayer was something about which she had a great deal of passion ("passionnante," in her own words). Our instructor listened momentarily but appeared to give the statement no further measure of attentiveness before simply proceeding with the scheduled curriculum.

If you choose to imagine Agnes #23 standing in front of the class, waving her stylus repeatedly before her, and speaking in a manner that suggested it was of absolutely no consequence whether her audience consisted of one or fifty, you may gain some measure of our own experience as we sat there listening and watching her move about.

Apparently, Dr. Leonard was aware of numerous studies that had "scientifically established" the usefulness of prayer. Whether it is energy, belief, or the intervention of the Universe itself, is apparently undetermined by these studies but what is clear is that prayer appears to have a considerable influence in hastening one's recovery, or at the very least in diminishing one's suffering. It was this kind of research that Dr. Leonard chose to build upon with his own unique investigation.

Agnes interjected, "Whether Dr. Leonard was purposely trying to research the topic of time remains unclear, but what is clear is that is exactly what he did!" Agnes bobbed about and excitedly exclaimed: "This is truly an amazing discovery, and remains almost completely unknown to those hindered by space-time!"

George pondered aloud, "Is it possible that Dr. Leonard and his research were under the influence of a time traveler?"

The statement caused Agnes's movements to come to an abrupt stop. Clearly, she had not considered the possibility before. She appeared to muse upon the prospect for only a moment before disallowing it all together. "It is of no matter to our discussion. Let us continue." She then proceeded to inform us that Rabin Medical Center was an enormous facility and had diagnosed more than 3,000 patients with "bloodstream infection" – an illness she had aptly described at the start. It was this very group that Dr. Leonard chose to employ in his study, without their awareness or knowledge. The group was separated into one half which was prayed for and one half which was not. "This all took place in the ATL of July 2000, and the research project was described as 'remote, retroactive intercessory prayer,'" Agnes added for our benefit.

"Here are the results for those who received the prayers!" She proceeded to the board and wrote each of the following as she spoke:

"Fever significantly less."

"Stay in hospital significantly less."

"Death of patients less."

After twice underlining each of the reported outcomes, she turned back to the class and waited for our reaction. It was Emanuel who first questioned the entire matter before us.

"How does this case history relate to the issue of time?" he asked. (I must admit possessing the very same thought myself.)

Agnes responded with certainty, "Because the patients in the study had been in the hospital ten years earlier! Dr. Leonard had randomly obtained names of individuals from the past and it had been those very individuals who had been prayed for in Dr. Leonard's present. When the patients' histories were examined, it became clear that even though they had been hospitalized years before, their outcomes were much more favorable than those who had not received prayer." She took account of the blank faces staring back at her before adding for additional edification, "The results of this study mean that time has no bearing whatsoever on the act of prayer."

"I still do not understand." Manuela #64 remained somewhat confused.

Agnes spoke with authority, "All 3,000 patients had been in the hospital in the past but only the half receiving prayer in the present obtained scientifically measurable positive results – results that were verified by the records of their patient histories." She tapped her stylus repeatedly with the words that followed, "Although he may never have become cognizant of the fact, Dr. Leonard proved beyond any doubt that time is without meaning and that the only moment is NOW."

It was after the Dr. Leonard discussion that I found occasion to return to the Akasha. I explained to Agnes #23 that I wished to see how my activities and interactions with Edward VIII had rectified timelines XXV and LII. Although the statement certainly contained an element of truth, it obviously was not my only rationale for seeking a return trip to the library. Nonetheless, Agnes was simply overjoyed with my initiative and even discussed the possibility of my receiving "extra credit" in terms of the coursework. It was this very premise of reviewing rectified timelines that permitted the discussion I had with Emmett not long thereafter.

We stood near the center of the chamber. I observed several apparent journeyman Wayfarers moving about and reading various volumes at further ends of the passageways and I could not help but notice an attractive-looking Mediterranean girl glance in my direction. Emmett confirmed his statement from our previous encounter, just as the young woman disappeared down one of the book corridors:

"There is no longer any doubt. The official records have been modified." We were far enough distant from the others so that he could speak without fear of being heard, "The ATL has been changed without proper approval."

I did not wish to appear ignorant but I could not help but ask, "What does that mean? I understand the record has been changed but what is the consequence of such a change?"

"Do you understand that everything done by the League is under the oversight of the Core?"

"I do."

He sounded grave, "This is problematic for many reasons. Everything in accordance with the ATL is approved by the Core . . . a group of nine. Sara #11, as Governor-General must sign off on any changes to the approved timeline before it is finalized and becomes a portion of 'that which will be.'"

"'And 'that which will be' guides the entire workings of the League?"

"Correct. Somehow, someone . . . or more than one," the old man added quickly, "has found a way to circumvent the oversight of the entire Core."

"Why would someone commence such an undertaking?"

Emmett quickly replied, "There are some who have grown very weary of the work we attempt to accomplish." Seeing my confusion, he added: "Assume you are a time traveler and wish to control history for yourself. You simply choose as your target someone with influence or authority – obviously, the individual would need to be someone with whom you had an affinity," he added. "With this approach, a time traveler could make changes to accomplish anything desired within the Collective Illusion. Any pursuit, any aspiration, anything imaginable becomes conceivable. There is nothing that one could not make possible."

"What has changed within the ATL?"

Emmett looked about, making certain that we were still alone. When he became satisfied we could discuss the matter further, he grasped his white beard in hand and looked upon me with all manner of seriousness, "You are familiar with Jamestown, and the landing in 1607?"

"Of course!" I answered swiftly.

"The ATL now indicates that Elizabeth I sent explorer Francis Drake to the west coast of the New World in 1577. The records indicate he landed at Oregon and then sailed south to California."

"To what end?"

"I have given the matter a great deal of thought." Emmett was somber, looking older than he had appeared previously. "Do you know who is considered the most powerful woman in the history of the world?"

"I do not," I confessed.

"Elizabeth I," Emmett replied. "It would seem that the Queen has chosen to expand the British empire by means of colonization one generation before the original timeline. I fear this is only the first of many changes to come."

"Then we must inform the Core – someone is altering the ATL."

"We cannot!" Emmett spoke with certainty, "We can tell no one."

I found myself astounded by his remark, "I do not understand."

He looked weary, "If you were changing the ATL without authorization, and someone became aware of what you were doing, what is to prevent you from making certain that individual is no longer a threat . . . no longer able to interfere with your intentions?"

"But surely you and members of the Core are aware of everything that changes within the timeline records?"

Emmett quickly disagreed, "That is not the case. Any change to the ATL becomes a part of the approved timeline. No one is made aware of such a change unless they are looking for it but I am talking about a far greater threat than the modification of the approved timeline."

"I do not understand."

Emmett looked about nervously, "Everyone within this facility no longer finds themselves subject to the Collective Illusion of time."

"Understood."

"But if you removed the individual from the League . . . if you went back to the moment of their recruitment and stopped it from occurring in the first place, it would be as if they were never here. And if they were never here, all memories of their presence would be eradicated. Such a change would go undetected." Emmett looked upon me with extreme unease, "The immensity of such a change is so complete that even the one responsible would no longer be aware that it had even taken place. You or I would simply disappear, and no one would know we had ever been here. No one!"

"Who is capable of such?"

"There are ten individuals who could make such things possible."

I looked at him inquisitively.

Emmett appeared extremely cautious but continued, "The Keeper of the Records and nine others."

"The Core?"

The old man nodded in the affirmative.

"Ben #239, are you with us?" Agnes was obviously irritated, having to repeat herself for the third time, "Ben #239 are you still there?"

It was the repetition of my name that finally brought me back to the classroom. "I apologize," I finally managed to say. "I was thinking about the coursework."

"That is all well and good," Agnes responded, "but right now it is your turn to read from the text." She shook her head, reopened her book to the page in question, and repeated her initial request, "Begin at the top of page 114."

Following her instruction, I read aloud, "The illusion of time and space came into existence with the inception of Moment One. Beyond the Collective Illusion, however, there is no time, there is no space; these have simply been created through the activities of the finite mind. It remains a challenge for those residing within physical consciousness to see beyond that which confronts them every instant of their lives. Throughout recorded history, one illusory restraint after another has been enacted to bind the perception of humankind to that which does not exist beyond the confines of what they have come to believe . . . "

"Okay, stop there," Agnes interrupted. She placed her text upon the desk, took stylus in hand, and proceeded to the board. "One of the questions on the midterm will be to describe in detail at least three 'restraints' that continue to empower the illusion of time. Does anyone remember one from our previous discussions?"

Several hands rose up in the air, and Agnes #23 pointed her stylus toward Emanuel.

"The calendar is one such restraint," he replied matter-of-factly.

"Continue," Agnes waved for him to proceed.

"We have given the calendar the very meaning we ascribe to it. It is only such because we have decided it so. When Pope Gregory XIII replaced the calendar from Caesar's time with that of the Gregorian in 1582, the date changed from Thursday, October the fourth, to Friday the fifteenth in the course of one solitary day. Ten days vanished simply because of his proclamation that it be done. Only perception has given any meaning to the value of a calendar."

I found myself nodding in appreciation of Emanuel's consistent ability to reiterate details covered within our class curriculum.

"Good!" Agnes bobbed about in agreement, as she wrote "Calendar" on the board and underlined it twice. She turned and provided us with a notable caveat, "Obviously, we have to use some scheduled timetable here at the school otherwise the entire curriculum would be taught at once, which would be absolutely overwhelming to each of you! Who else has a restraint?"

"Señora?" Manuela #64 waved an arm, calling attention to herself. "We also examined the matter of 'time zones.'"

"Exactly!" Agnes agreed, writing the two words on the board, "And what an interesting history they provide for our discussion!" She whipped her stylus through the air and began to recall the various misleading restraints that had impacted the subject of time zones: "We have the equatorial line at Ciudad Mitad del Mundo in Ecuador. We have the creation of Greenwich Mean Time. We have the use of the chronometer for maritime travel. We have the Railway Time Convention of 1883. We have the various renditions of the International Date Line . . . imagine, believing you could stand over an imaginary line and have the opportunity to place one foot in Monday and the other in Tuesday. What foolishness!" She shook her head in disbelief, only stopping as another thought came to her:

"Does anyone know which country comes closest to understanding the illusory nature of these time zone restraints?" Agnes looked about, seeing only blank faces before her. Hearing no response, she added, "In spite of a landmass covering five time zones, they subscribe to the existence of only one time throughout the entire country. Can anybody name that country? Anybody?"

There was only silence.

Agnes wrote the solution on the board, "The answer is China; they call it Beijing Time." As was her favored form of emphasis, "China" was underlined twice. "You know," Agnes reflected aloud, "it is the Chinese perception of there being only one time – 'Beijing Time' – that actually comes closest to reflecting the reality of the only moment being NOW."

"Okay, who remembers a third restraint . . .?"

Bonne Soeur Marie #304 responded in French, "Une horloge," and then repeated in English, "A clock."

"Explain . . ." Agnes #23 waved the stylus in her direction.

As the class discussion continued, my thoughts turned once again to Ruth #7, Emmett, and the very possibility of everything transpiring since the moment of my recruitment somehow becoming eradicated.

It is an ironic discovery for every Time Traveler to suddenly ascertain that the very question which motivated life in the Collective Illusion remains the very same in a world without time: "Who Am I?" This query has empowered both thought and activity from the inception of Moment One and forever remains a part of personal awareness wherever you may find yourself.

It is this quest to find an answer that enables each individual to discover the true Self. And, ultimately, it is only the true Self who will serve as legitimate heir to the Consciousness of the Whole, which forever remains our collective destiny.

Excerpt, "Perceiving the Self," *A Time Traveler's Code of Conduct* **by Ruth #7**

FIVE: *Journal Entry – April 13 ATL*

I have chosen to include herein those classes, conversations, and instances that may best illustrate my own experience since being admitted to the League school. Perchance the next occasion of note began with Agnes #23 throwing her arms in the air (nearly losing her grasp on the stylus) while exclaiming with theatrical intensity, "It is a wonder that the human creature remains so blinded from reality! The truth is all about them. Why do they refuse to look?"

Although the question had been directed toward the five of us, it seemed entirely rhetorical in nature, therefore requiring no response.

"Every culture has stories and legends and fables that elucidate the illusion of time. These tales have amazing similarities but no one ever bothers to ask, 'Why?' Why do these legends exist the world over in the first place, and what do they suggest about the nature of time?"

Again, the question appeared rhetorical, and Agnes confirmed as much when she continued without waiting for a reply: "Today, let us look at the Japanese story of Urashima." She eyed each of us closely, as though to emphasize her next point: "Let me assure you that we could just as easily discuss the legend of Urashimako, from a thousand years before, or we could go back even earlier to the Hindu epic of Mahabharata, or we might go into a more recent perception of the past and hear the tale of Rip Van Winkle. Each of these makes it exceedingly clear that time is not a constant, nor is it unaffected by personal perception." She tapped her stylus in our direction before finally acknowledging my roomie, who had suddenly begun waving his hand in the air.

"Yes, George #111?"

"Isn't Rip Van Winkle simply a child's tale?" he asked.

"Is it?" Agnes responded in turn, eyeing him intensely, "Or is it instead a reflection of some truth about time?"

As I was completely unfamiliar with the tale, I had nothing to add to the discussion but unfamiliarity with a subject was not an impediment to Agnes's method of instruction, prompting her to inquire, "Ben #239, what do you think these tales suggest about the nature of time?"

I readily confessed that which came immediately to mind, "I am unacquainted with these stories but as time is an illusion and as its perception is tied to the one observing it, I would imagine each tale illustrates how the passage of time may be very different for the primary character than for anyone else involved."

"Exactly!" Agnes slapped the top of her desk with her free hand, providing us a mode of emphasis we had not witnessed previously. The lesson continued: "Rip Van Winkle fell asleep for only a moment but woke up to discover that twenty years have passed. In the Jewish tale of Choni Hameagel, our hero falls asleep and awakens to discover his entire village changed in the 70 years that have ensued. In the epic of Mahabharata, the king travels to the abode of Brahma to hear a 20-minute story and when he returns comes to the realization that he has been gone for millions of years. I want you to understand that in each of these tales the character is essentially unaffected by the passage of time. Time appears to have the capacity to alter everything else but the individual who is the focus of the story; that individual remains unchanged. Time does not exist for those who remain outside of it. The Collective Illusion that blinds the rest of the world has no impact. This fact is central to understanding the story of Urashima."

Agnes approached the board and wrote, "Urashima," underlining it twice, before turning in our direction and continuing: "Obviously, there are multiple versions of the tale, but this one is my favorite. In the story, we have a young fisherman named Urashima who stops a group of children from tormenting a small turtle." Agnes #23 cupped her hands to provide further clarity as to the size of said turtle, before adding, "Urashima saves the turtle and allows it to return to the ocean. Now what these children were unable to see in their own blindness is that in reality, this turtle is a princess – a fact that is made quite clear when Urashima is taken beneath the sea to a beautiful kingdom on the ocean floor. In this place, Urashima sees things as they truly are. He is then rewarded by the princess's father, the emperor of the sea himself." Agnes bobbed about while assuring us, "The symbolism in this tale is simply amazing!"

My roomie looked at me inquisitively, as if to inquire, "What does she mean?" and I shook my head, indicating that it was best not to ask.

Agnes continued the story: "He stays in the kingdom for three days, at which point the princess gives him a mysterious box, assuring him he will retain the safety of the kingdom wherever he goes, as long as the box is never opened. When his experience in the undersea kingdom has come to an end, he returns home only to find that 100 years have passed for the rest of the world. Urashima is the same as he was before the journey began but everyone else he knew has died due to the passage of time. Unfortunately, Urashima misses the beauty of the kingdom he has left behind, and he is saddened that all those he knew from the past are gone. In his dismay, he opens the box and, in an instant, ages 100 years himself."

Agnes #23 looked about the classroom to gauge the response of each of us before asking, "What do you think this means?"

It was Emanuel #41 who seemed to be the first to grasp the message of the tale, "When Urashima was under the sea, he was no longer blinded by the Collective Illusion. The emperor's kingdom is not impacted by space-time. In this place, one may see things as they truly are. I believe the illusion of time has been trapped within the box. Even when he returns, Urashima is not personally affected by the Collective Illusion. Everything around him is influenced by time but not Urashima. At least not until he opens the box."

"Excellent!" Agnes pointed her stylus in his direction. "It was Urashima himself who gave life to the illusion. Had it not been for his actions, he would have retained the safety of the kingdom and the cessation of the Collective Illusion upon himself from that point forward . . . and that is exactly what each of you must learn to do. It is really that simple. The kingdom under the sea is not affected by things in the physical world, just as we are unaffected and quite safe here at the school – safe from everything that impacts the illusion of time."

Agnes #23 nodded with complete satisfaction, but I could not help but wonder if her words were no longer true.

It came as quite a surprise for myself as well as my four classmates to discover that we were to have a "guest speaker" later that same day. Agnes gave the announcement toward the end of the morning session with a lack of fanfare suggesting our instructor was not eager to pass control of the curriculum to anyone. Still, it seemed a welcome relief to be offered some variety in the manner of our instruction. Nevertheless, that relief soon turned to disappointment when the awaited guest arrived in the form of two visitors from the Core (Emma #119 and Milton #71), and the topic of the scheduled discourse was announced as an examination of the "League Disciplinary Process." Our guest speakers sat side by side on stools positioned in front of the class. Each held onto several pieces of paper, which I assumed contained lecture notes or some semblance of an outline.

Emma #119 peered over her black-rimmed spectacles and provided the class with the primary rationale for having such a procedure in the first place: "After having undertaken at least one timeline mission . . ." she turned momentarily to look upon Agnes in the corner of the room who nodded to confirm the accuracy of the statement, "it is appropriate that we discuss the League's disciplinary process. We have found that the capacity to alter the illusion of space-time has occasionally, for some, become an unfortunate temptation. It is regrettable that a few Wayfarers – graduates from this very school – have succumbed to the temptation. Even some of our students have occasionally chosen to circumvent a number of the rules." The last statement was followed by a thorough peering over her glasses, as she took occasion to look suspiciously upon each of the five of us. "It is for this reason that the 'League Disciplinary Process' is reviewed with every incoming class."

Milton came next. His English clothing and manner of speech caused him to appear more dapper and cheerful than seemed appropriate for our chosen topic of conversation: "There are time travel protocols that we take very seriously here. You will find a complete listing in the appendix of your text but, as you may know, these include such things as not following the instruction of your classroom teacher or supervisor, ignoring the directive of a member of the Core, refusing an assignment from the ATL Mission Office, personal time excursions that have no bearing upon your mission, and revisiting periods in your personal timeline for rectification of any issue for which you desire an alternate outcome."

Emma was quick to add for our clarification: "Please note that the listing is not meant to be all-inclusive and for that reason contains the statement, 'Things also not specified on this list that any other reasonably-minded Wayfarer would find unethical.'"

Milton glanced at the paper held within his hands and proceeded with the first measure of disciplinary action: "The first violation of any time travel protocols will result in a written warning."

Emma stated the second violation without requiring an examination of her notes: "The consequence of a second violation will result in the confiscation of your Horologium for at least two weeks, resulting in the inability to time travel. Depending upon the nature of your violation, this time period may be extended."

It was Milton's turn, "For a third violation, in addition to the confiscation of your Horologium, a month-long probation from all League activities will result, including the Akasha library and League café, and a permanent record will be placed in your personnel file."

"A fourth violation," Emma declared, "will result in the confiscation of your Horologium and expulsion from the League until such time as a complete investigation and hearing can take place. Should such investigation prove that you have deliberately violated time travel protocols on all four occasions, you will be permanently expelled from the League and your Horologium will be destroyed. You will be returned to your personal timeline one hour *after* your point of recruitment for the process of personal eradication due to natural causes." She looked gravely upon the class before her, "In this way, we remain cognizant of your behavior and former presence, while still managing to eliminate the opportunity for you to create any further disturbance."

Milton interjected, "The consequence of personal eradication shall also result for any capital offense against the League, the authorized timeline, or such an offense against any other individual, living or dead, in recorded history – whether past or future."

Emma #119 peered over her spectacles while stating, "It should be noted that upon approval of the Governor-General anyone suspected of a serious violation of time travel protocols may be tracked at any time without their knowledge or consent as a means of corroborating such violation." She looked out upon each of us as if to discover who might already be contemplating such an offense while asking, "Do you have any questions?"

It was quickly apparent that there would be none.

Truly, it was a welcome relief for the class to have Manuela #64 next up on our scheduled agenda. The occasion marked her personal deliberation of the assignment detailing child labor and the rectification of the issue within the ATL. Although she had commented previously on her preference for written assignments and an apparent dread of speaking in public in general – noting that the Akasha itself recorded such as one of the top five fears in existence (the others being death, heights, spiders, and being subjected to another's judgment) – she stood at the front of the room, her dark hair pulled back and braided behind her head. She held a couple of small papers within one hand and appeared cautiously ready to share her experience. (Agnes #23 sat near the front of the room, seemingly at the ready to grade the presentation we were about to witness.)

I noted immediately that Manuela required neither stylus nor the board to fully explain the assignment, and I would come to find her discussion of the issue truly enlightening, illuminating a problem of which I had gone previously unaware. While choosing not to provide an excessive dialogue of "background information" as was the favored approach of our regular instructor,

Manuela instead imparted only enough details for our comprehension of the mission as well as her part in it.

As I understand it, the issue of child labor had become a dilemma during – what came to be called – "the industrial revolution." Younglings who had not yet seen the age of six were often employed day and night in positions for which they received a meager wage, all the while being forced to take part in grueling and dangerous vocations. They served as "spinners" in cotton mills, and "oyster shuckers" in seaports, and underground "miners" in search of coal and such, and "laborers" in every manner of factory. To be sure, there were those against such an obvious misuse of children (who might be better served with schooling and some semblance of education) and tried to bring the matter to public attention but far too many others had come to rely on this cheapest form of labor and often went to great lengths to conceal it. Herein was the essential problem.

Manuela #64 told us of two individuals championing the reform of such immoral exploitation who had received some measure of recognition, in return, for their efforts: Edgar Gardner Murphy, a minister, and Lewis Hine, a photographer – an occupation of which I had no previous awareness until Manuela clarified the profession as part of her preliminary explanation. I choose here to include some of her own words as a means of clarifying her part in the assignment:

"Edgar Gardner Murphy was an advocate of children who could not speak for themselves," she said proudly. From the tone of her words and the manner of her speech, it was evident that Manuela possessed a great deal of understanding for her timeline target, "Although he lived to be only 43, he became responsible for much social change in this matter of children and their wellbeing." She continued, "His father had abandoned the family when he was only five. His mother remained busy running a boarding house and providing for the family. It was for this reason that much of his schooling and encouragement came from the Episcopal Church. Is it any wonder that Edgar himself became a priest? The Church would become his greatest source of support and my own challenge within timeline XIV."

Manuela went on to describe how Edgar would become well-loved in every congregation he had served – in Texas, New York, Ohio, and Alabama. She detailed how the problem within timeline XIV was that he had remained a priest for the remainder of his life, never involving himself with the concern at hand.

"When I visited his past, I discovered that in addition to the Church, he possessed a love for writing. As a priest, he had used this ability in the creation of his sermons but the approved timeline confirmed that the talent he possessed was far greater."

As the five of us had come to know the backgrounds and life existence of one another, it was exceedingly clear that Manuela #64 had often penned leaflets and pamphlets in her own work in South America, where she had found occasion to focus on independence and the rightful place of women.

"In 1900, I helped Edgar become aware of the fact that one-fourth of all textile workers in Alabama were not yet sixteen. These children were paid one-tenth the wage of an adult! Just disgraceful!" She added, "Edgar was very upset by this situation. I inspired him to use writing as a means of calling the issue to public attention. Using both passion and the written word, he persuaded the Alabama legislature to advance a bill that would prohibit employment for anyone under the age of twelve. Businesses intervened, causing the bill's defeat, but the defeat motivated him to help create the Alabama Child Labor Committee. With its success, Edgar next proposed the creation of a National Child Labor Committee to be headquartered in New York."

She looked briefly toward Agnes #23 (who remained busily occupied with the taking of notes) before continuing: "Once the National Child Labor Committee was started, it came to the attention of Lewis Hine, a photographer, who believed that the problem could best be brought to the country's attention with pictures of these children performing their labors. Originally, Lewis had been educated as both a teacher and photographer and had often documented the condition of immigrants as they came to the United States. He believed that photography could be used for social reform."

Manuela paused for a moment before adding her own involvement in the situation, "It was simple, really, to inspire him to turn his work toward these children. Unfortunately, photography was absolutely prohibited in factories and mills and mines, so Hine would disguise himself as a salesman, or a factory inspector, or a vendor of some sort or another to gain admission, giving him the opportunity to take pictures." She distributed the two small pages she had been holding within her hand, describing them as "examples of Hine's work." One showed the photograph of a young girl who worked as a "spinner" in a mill; the other was of two small boys in a cave, soiled from head to foot, as their occupation was "miners."

"It was the creation of these committees, Edgar's writing, Lewis Hine's pictures, and the distribution of tens of thousands of pamphlets throughout the country that resulted in laws bringing an end to this problem of child labor. I am truly proud that I had the ability to work with Edgar Gardner Murphy and Lewis Hines, and I am grateful that the mission assignment has been rectified within the ATL."

She concluded by adding, "The end."

As soon as the words were spoken, George, Emanuel, Bonne Soeur Marie, and I applauded with enthusiasm, prompting Manuela #64 to smile and say simply, "Gracias."

As a means of celebrating both the completion and narrative of Manuela's mission assignment, we five found occasion to journey to the League café for some respite and merrymaking. To be sure, as any form of alcohol was prohibited for at least twelve hours prior to a time traveler's excursion, the café lacked any form of libation common at the taverns I had once frequented. Nonetheless, the coffee was always fresh and those who preferred could find an adequate selection of tea, and there was always a considerable choice of something to eat. (I choose here to admit my own fondness for the café's assortment of muffins and honey.)

As we entered the café, I immediately came face-to-face with the attractive Mediterranean girl from the library. She appeared near the same age as my current younger self, and as she passed on her way out of the café, I nodded, causing her to smile and say only, "Hi."

My roomie, George, took occasion to push his elbow deep into my side, whispering in a low voice, "I think she likes you."

I chose to ignore his remark, as I noticed Sara #11 sitting at a table with an elderly man who had his back to us. The appearance of such fine gray hair made it quickly apparent that the gentleman was none other than Grimwald #94, Elder professor and member of the Core. Sara was doing the talking while Grimwald nodded frequently in apparent agreement. He was listening intently to her words, drinking from his mug only on occasion. As the two conversed, I led the class to the front of the café line so that we might procure our chosen provisions. By the time we had all gathered a refreshment, the Governor-General had left the café, leaving Grimwald by himself.

It was I who proposed to my classmates that we might choose the opportunity to sit with him. When there came ready accord, I approached the professor and suggested as much. His kind face gave way to agreement, prompting each of us to take a seat. Emanuel spoke first and explained the occasion of our gathering, "Manuela #64 just finished discussing her mission assignment."

"Very good! I am most interested," Grimwald took a sip from his mug, appearing genuinely intrigued as he looked in Manuela's direction. "Tell me about it."

Having already detailed the essentials of Manuela's mission, I will not go into particulars here other than to suggest that she provided an abbreviated but inclusive discussion of the very assignment she had just reviewed for us. Once she had finished, I found it agreeable and surprising that Grimwald took occasion to ask the rest of the class what each was working on.

Emanuel #41 elected to go next: "I am rectifying a problem that postponed the Methodist spiritual movement." Emanuel provided further clarification for anyone to whom the matter was unknown, "This all took place during the Collective Illusion of the eighteenth century. My two primary targets are John Wesley and George Whitefield. According to the ATL, their religious fervor will inspire a spiritual renewal across two countries. The problem is that several timelines indicate both jealousy and disagreement between them will undermine the entire movement. I plan to have it resolved within several days."

"That sounds very interesting," Elder Professor Grimwald #94 responded with complete sincerity.

It was Bonne Soeur Marie #304 who followed. Whether it was due to Grimwald's position on the Core or Bonne Soeur Marie's modesty in such situations I could not say but she appeared to blush with her words, "I often work with healing." However, she became much more comfortable with that which ensued:

"My target is Hippocrates. Hippocrates has been called the 'Father of Medicine,' as he was the first to establish medicine as a learned profession. An educated Greek man, he taught his students that disease was the result of an individual's activities, diet, and habits. Before that, many believed illness was a punishment from the gods," she added for our benefit. "The problem is that during his own upbringing and education he took part in countless athletic activities and would devote much of his life to training for these events. Hippocrates becomes an athlete in at least four timelines, which postpones the establishment of medicine for multiple generations. This is the problem I need to fix."

Grimwald nodded enthusiastically, "A most excellent assignment!"

The professor's words were sincere, giving every indication that he was interested in all that was being said. Truly, I found myself liking this member of the Core.

It was my roomie who insisted I go next, and so I proceeded to describe my own outing, which entailed interactions with two kings, two mistresses, and a prime minister. I also took occasion to repeat the admiration I felt for the Akasha library, as the records themselves had so thoroughly detailed all that I had encountered.

When I had completed the tale, Grimwald acknowledged his own fascination with the library and suggested that my mission was "well done," adding that on several of his personal assignments he had found occasion to interact with royalty, "I have definitely met my share of crowned heads," he acknowledged.

George #111 went last. "My strength is working with philanthropy and helping those who are underprivileged." He interjected, "Emmett has told me that the word philanthropy is Greek and describes a 'love of humanity,' so that is how I see it. Already I have had missions inspiring individuals with substantial means. My current mission is really a 'background mission' to learn more about the Islamic pillar of Zakat. For centuries it has been the practice of setting aside money for those in need and has helped the poor, those in debt, and individuals who are sick or unable to care for themselves. By learning more about how Zakat began, I may be better prepared for my own work as a Wayfarer."

Grimwald was very supportive, "I often thought my own background missions were as interesting as timeline assignments."

Without a doubt, I found the conversation between the six of us enjoyable. Grimwald was a man with whom I felt comfortable. My sense of relaxation prompted me to speak further, "We have met you, and Sara #11, and both Milton #71 and Emma #119 have already given us a guest presentation about the 'League Disciplinary Process.'"

Grimwald's kindly face turned to a grimace as he

made light of the matter, "I imagine that was both an uplifting and enjoyable presentation?"

I smiled and continued, "Who are the others in the Core?"

The professor took a sip from his mug and spoke without reservation: "Well, there is Hina #407, who is a wonderful woman and was in my original recruitment class . . ." he added for edification. "There is Hakim #60 – at six-foot-eight, you will find him the tallest among us. Let's see, there is Lucius #19, and . . ." He appeared to ponder the names he had already mentioned before coming up with, "Mia #161, and of course Ruth #7, who wrote your text."

The ease with which he spoke gave me nerve enough to say, "I have been hoping to see Ruth #7, as she was responsible for my recruitment. Ever since my arrival, I have wanted the opportunity to speak with her further. When do you think that might be possible?"

Grimwald looked at me inquisitively and seemed to be contemplating the best response. He certainly looked as if he wished to say more. He moved to say something and then abruptly stopped, taking a sip from his mug instead. For an instant, he looked nervously about the café before finally choosing to reply with: "I have long admired Ruth but perhaps this is something you need to discuss with Sara #11?"

With that, he placed his mug upon the table, rose from his seat, excused himself from our group, and hastily left the room.

It was Manuela #64 who chose to describe his hasty departure, "That seems most peculiar."

As a member of the League, you will find that a total shift in personal consciousness is inevitable. Your recruitment will change your perception of the world around you. After all, from the moment of your first breath, each of your experiences has been measured by the space-time illusion. Every event and all of your individual activities have been planned around that which does not ultimately exist. Collective humanity has come to accept that "in such and such a time" the seasons unfold, historical events are noted, one's birthday occurs, the sun rises, there is a time for every manner of activity. The list goes on without end.

Know that this shift in consciousness does not come without some personal regret, for although humankind has often feared the end of time, a world without time may be harder for some to face. When you find yourself out of time, all too quickly you will see that everyone and everything you have ever loved remains bounded by an experience to which you are no longer connected. And before that realization is made totally comforted within yourself there arises an even greater challenge – how are you going to account for the Eternity that has been given you?

Excerpt, "Introduction Orientation," *A Time Traveler's Code of Conduct* **by Ruth #7**

SIX: *Journal Entry – April 16 ATL*

Not too many days hence, I found the opportunity to take Emmett into my confidence in the matter of my Horologium. The outcome of the interaction between us, however, became far different than anything I had imagined. After I had explained the matter of the etching within the watch and he had procured information from the various records within the Akasha for himself, Emmett's response, "This is but a portion of the story," appeared neither appropriate nor helpful.

I stood before him and again explained the issue of my timepiece: "Within the cover of the mechanism is the lettering 'Help!R7.' It is right here!" I held the watch in my hand and (after confirming that no one was looking in our direction) lifted it to his eyes to afford a closer inspection.

"I understand completely." The old man remained patient but firm, "I am telling you this is only part of the story. The records indicate that the inscription within your Horologium has yet to occur."

I lowered it, looked upon the lettering for myself, shook my head in confusion, and restored the timepiece to its proper place within my pocket.

"I do not understand," was all I managed to say.

"I have examined the Akasha. It is clear that this matter of the etching within your Horologium *will occur* but it is also quite evident that it has *yet to occur*."

"It remains beyond my comprehension to grasp what you are suggesting."

Emmett explained, "It is clearly evident that you received a timepiece from Ruth containing the etching you now possess. However, it is just as apparent from the records themselves that Ruth has yet to make such an engraving within your watch."

"I find myself completely confused."

The old man's patience continued, "Since the Akasha indicates that the matter of the inscription within your watch has yet to occur, it will occur sometime *after* your arrival . . . sometime after this very moment."

I reflected upon the matter before concluding, "My confusion has not abated."

Emmett posed the query, "Why would Ruth choose

you as the one to relay such information?"

"I know not," was all that would come to me.

"Perhaps it was you who encouraged Ruth to write within your Horologium?"

When I did not move to respond, Emmett spoke as if there could be no doubt: "The answer is clear. At some point, you will return to the occasion of your own recruitment and persuade Ruth to make the inscription before she gives you the timepiece. It would appear that the entire matter was your idea . . . there can be no other explanation."

It took a moment to fully understand what he was saying but once my mind gave way to clarity, it provided the most wonderful thought, "By so doing, I may find occasion to ask why she requires my assistance, to begin with."

Emmett shook his head in the negative, "Such would not be advisable."

"Can you explain?"

"From the records, it appears that Ruth has managed to keep her thoughts concealed, as there is no indication of whom or of what she has grown concerned. Perhaps whoever is behind the cause of Ruth's distress remains uncertain as to just what she knows. Ruth's involvement in this matter is extremely unclear. Should she verbalize the individual who is the cause of her concern, at that moment it will become a part of the records."

I considered the entire situation before us. Perhaps it was the thoroughness of my own classroom instruction that enabled me to perceive complications within the practice of time travel about which I had been previously unaware: "The individual behind this may have found themselves with a substantial dilemma."

Emmett motioned toward me, "What are you thinking?"

"Ruth is the author of our text. The entire curriculum is based on her words. If Ruth were to be eradicated, what might happen to the school? What might happen to all those who have undergone previous instruction? What might transpire within the League itself?"

Emmett added, "What might happen to the ATL itself, and all of the timeline adjustments that have already been rectified?"

"Truly, such a question is enormous to consider!"

After discussing the matter further, and taking sufficient time to review my proposed interaction with Ruth, I counseled that there appeared to be no point in delaying such an excursion. The course of action was quite clear and I was confident of the mission's intent. As such matters were resolved, I took hold of the Horologium and moved the hands counterclockwise. I then gave thought to the situation, stated my own name aloud thrice over, pressed the button, and breathed.

I underwent the sensation of falling at least twice as long as that experienced on the excursion to the British King but much shorter than on my journey to Ramesses. I soon found myself within the very bedchamber I had once occupied, at first hovering within the frame of the old man in his bed. It became readily apparent that an individual within the throws of demise did not possess as great a hold upon the traveler's vaporous self as an individual whose life force remained very much intact. I moved from the bed, stood up, and watched as my grandsons departed for their sustenance.

On the table next to the bedside, I could see the Dryden essay I had read some time before, along with my pocketbook and two keys. Yes, this was my room. I took a moment to savor each of the happenings that had transpired since the day of my recruitment when all at once I found myself as spectator to the ghostly form of the pretty, young Ruth materializing before me.

Clearly aware of my presence, she appeared stunned and quickly inquired, "Who are you?"

"I am he who you seek." I pointed toward the old man lying in bed. She looked upon me with much confusion, prompting me to add, "Emmett sent me."

Ruth retained her look of bewilderment asking only, "Why is this happening?"

"There is the matter of my timepiece," I said matter-of-factly. I handed her my mechanism, making certain that the issue of its engraving was before her.

After looking it over with some measure of fascination, Ruth handed it back to me. She then took the selfsame Horologium which was to be mine from her pocket and showed me that its internal-facing was without lettering.

"I am indeed in need of assistance," she said finally, "and it remains most unclear as to who can be trusted." As she spoke, the old man in his bed began to move and sighed with some degree of discomfort, causing her to advise, "We must act quickly."

She glanced about the room, noticing my keys upon the table, and moved swiftly to procure one. I found myself astonished that her ghostly form could take hold of such a physical object. The amazement upon my face prompted her to state, "It becomes possible with practice." I watched as she inscribed the lettering upon the watch with the end of my own key.

As she looked upon me, it was quite evident that she wished to say more but instead affirmed in no uncertain terms, "You must go now."

A moment later I was gone, leaving Ruth #7 alone to undertake the very matter of my recruitment.

"We will discuss Asahi Takahashi's encounter with time," Agnes used her stylus to write the name on the board. "His experience demonstrates beyond any doubt, that time remains flexible, even for those trapped within its deception!" Our instructor bobbed excitedly about, while providing the necessary "background information" that was part of her tale.

"Asahi was an AI engineer in Hokuto City in the Collective Illusion of the twenty-third century . . ." Agnes stopped and added for our clarification, "AI has to do with computers, and robots, and machines that perform labor formerly undertaken by humans."

Her description prompted me to make a mental note to discuss the matter with my roomie, as it seemed conceivable that George might have encountered such on his excursion to the "Gates" mission.

"You see, Hokuto City had become the Asian continent's version of Silicon Valley."

To be sure, I did not "see," as the word "silicon" was unclear to me but I chose to let the matter go until I could find occasion to examine the word in question with my roomie.

"I should probably explain that at one time this whole area had been Japanese countryside. It overflowed with produce. You know, it was the center of wine-making for more than 200 years! Besides grapes, you could find peaches and cherries and strawberries and pears. In this very place there was a large Shinto shrine named Misogi . . . in any event," Agnes #23 pointed her stylus at each of us in turn, "By the time Asahi was a young man, this was not the Hokuto City he had come to know."

Agnes continued. "The city had grown to become a major metropolis. Most of the crops had moved to Hokkaido . . . I don't recall where they moved the shrine. In any event, Hokuto City was a busy place! They had a major technology center, all kinds of businesses, nearly as many skyscrapers as Tokyo itself, and the most amazing maglev train system throughout the entire city . . . it is a train that runs on magnets." Agatha took occasion to write "maglev = magnets" on the board for our clarification.

"On the morning of April 18, 2248, just as Asahi entered his place of employment, in one solitary instant it was as if everything before his eyes was suddenly transformed," our instructress leaned forward, squinting her eyes to provide some additional drama for our benefit. "He was no longer at Kawasaki Robotics, instead, he found himself standing in the Japanese countryside at the Misogi Shrine – a shrine that had not been there for over 100 years."

"Rather than skyscrapers and elevated trains, he was surrounded by trees, and grass, a large Koi pond with fish as large as your arm . . ." she moved her hands apart some distance to show us the size of the creatures, "and he stood in front of the most beautiful Shinto shrine with lovely wooden buildings, covered walkways, and ornate roofs."

"Asahi was amazed!" she nearly dropped the stylus with her excitement. "Remember, only a few moments before he had been at work! As he stood there in complete bewilderment, two Shinto priests came to speak with him. Although they were quite pleasant, they seemed somewhat amused by the metallic-looking clothing he wore . . . standard office attire, as far as Asahi was concerned." Agnes interjected, "He asked where he was, and they told him, Misogi Shrine, Hokuto

City. Asahi found this all so hard to believe! He asked them for the date, and do you know what they told him, 'April 18, 1992.' It was two hundred and fifty-six years to the day!"

"According to his own account, he spent more than an hour at the shrine . . . the priests even took him on a tour. Before his very eyes, he was able to see the area as it had once been. Somehow, he had escaped the Collective Illusion of the twenty-third century only to find himself in the illusion of the twentieth."

"When they had completed the tour, one of the priests was speaking to him about the history of the shrine and, as Asahi described it, all at once there appeared a bright 'flash of light' and in an instant, everything changed back as quickly as it had begun. Suddenly, he found himself sitting at his own workstation, returning to the illusion of his own space-time."

Our instructor bobbed about, waving her stylus before us. "You know, this whole story became quite popular in Japanese graphic novels. Asahi was never embarrassed by what he had seen. He was happy to tell his experience to anyone who would listen. In time, it became known as 'Asahi's April time slip.'"

She turned and wrote the words on the board, giving each an appropriate double underline.

When class resumed after the midday break, we found Agnes #23 even more animated than her usual self. She stood before us, muttering, bobbing about, and asserting just under her breath, "I cannot remember the last time such a thing occurred," and, "This is so exciting," and "I wonder why this is happening?" Her enthusiasm appeared to cause some measure of bewilderment as one moment she held the stylus in hand, the next tossing it upon her desk. She picked up her textbook to flip through its pages, then suddenly decided to put it back in place. She next turned to erase the board, admired her work, and then took occasion to erase it once again. The whole while, her mumbling went unabated, giving voice to, "I cannot believe it," and, "This will be so amazing!"

Although we had often borne witness to such excitability in her instruction, the drama before us was even more animated than that usually observed. It was Emanuel who finally gave expression to the spectacle before us:

"Is everything okay with you?"

Her movements came to an abrupt stop and Agnes appeared elated, "It is absolutely amazing! I am just so excited!"

Bonne Soeur Marie queried next, "Pourquoi . . . Why? Madame, what is it that is so exciting?"

Agnes tried hard to contain herself, she took hold of the stylus and waved it about with her joyful news: "There is to be a meeting of the Core! The WHOLE Core!" she said enthusiastically. "I cannot remember the last time something like this occurred. It is just so exciting!"

I interjected, "Why is the Core meeting?"

"Oh, I don't know," Agnes #23 responded, as though my query was of little import. "They will be here! I am sure we will hear more about it when they arrive. It is just so exciting!" She looked out over the class and confessed enthusiastically, "I just heard the news at lunch."

Although George #111 had been waving his hand about, rather than waiting to be noticed he inquired, "Why does the Core normally meet?"

The query appeared to cause her some measure of irritability, "I don't know . . . Core business, obviously." She shook her head in dismay. "The point is, they will be here!"

After moving about for a few moments more, she managed to regain some semblance of composure. She glanced about her desk as though looking for something before finally appearing to recall why we had gathered in the first place, "Oh yes, this afternoon we need to discuss the Omega Point." She moved to write the two words on the board, and while her back was to the class she added, "Obviously, I will provide the appropriate background information."

As our instructor faced the other away, George turned in my direction, silently mouthing the words, "Background information."

"Let me start," Agnes affirmed, "by telling you about the Jesuit priest who created the term. 'Omega Point.' His name was Pierre Teilhard de Chardin, and in spite of remaining trapped within the Collective Illusion for his entire life, he often glimpsed beyond it!" The statement was spoken in hushed words as though she was alerting us to some tremendous secret. "Some might say that he was a man ahead of his time."

Our instructress went on to describe the life of de Chardin, highlighting his many achievements, his global travels, and how his own Church had attempted to silence him. In addition to being a priest, he was a scientist, a philosopher, and a teacher. He came to believe that the entire universe was undergoing its own process of growth and evolution. According to Agnes, his written works brought him international attention. They also brought condemnation from the Catholic hierarchy. During his lifetime and even after his death, Rome banned his books with the justification that it was necessary in order to protect the minds of the uneducated and the young. Once the background was sufficient, Agnes pointed back to the words "Omega Point" on the board:

"It is a point in which everything comes together as one unified WHOLE." She waved her stylus in the form of a circle before us. "He believed that the entire universe was moving toward a higher level of consciousness – a point of integration that was the destiny of all Creation. Sounds very much like the consciousness that existed prior to Moment One . . . doesn't it?" She nodded in the affirmative. "Just as I have told you again and again – the truth is everywhere, so why do so many refuse to look for it?"

While the question still hung before us, a visitor intruded our class instruction, causing Agnes herself to come to a complete stop. All at once the Governor-General, Sara #11, poked her head in the doorway, asking that her interruption be excused, and stating without further explanation, "Agnes, I need to speak with Ben #239."

The eyes of my teacher opened as wide as my own. She turned to me and demanded (as though I had been caught committing some major offense): "Ben, the Governor-General wishes to see you NOW!"

As I got up from my seat, George quickly glanced in my direction, giving the impression of both concern and surprise. I admit feeling a measure of both as the Governor-General and I departed the classroom. Sara looked at me briefly, saying only, "Follow me."

Having been called to the headmaster's office in my boyhood on one occasion, I can vouch that this present journey toward the administrative offices felt very much the same as the one I had undertaken in my youth. Both were fraught with equal measures of anxiety and confusion, as in neither instance could I recollect what offense might have prompted such a meeting in the first place. The Governor-General said no more, and I heard only the sounds of our footsteps down the long, empty hallway. I had never made the trip before and (in spite of my own anxiety) made note of the various offices and doorways we passed: "Personnel," "Recruitment," "Student Services," "Meeting Room 1," Meeting Room 2," "Recordkeeping," "ATL Mission Office," and finally "Governor-General." To be sure, the trip felt longer than the distance we had traversed but the greater surprise came when I saw our Elder Professor, Grimwald #94, sitting in wait in her office upon our arrival.

A look of concern had replaced his former, kindly face: "Hello #239."

Sara pointed toward a seat for me to occupy and then took her own chair behind the desk. She came to the purpose of our gathering immediately, "Ben, I am concerned about you."

I managed to say, "What is your concern, Miss Sara?"

Sara looked briefly toward Grimwald, and turned back in my direction, "It has come to my attention that on at least two occasions you have inquired about Ruth #7 Would you like to tell me why?"

Her words took me by surprise but I confessed, "She was my recruiter . . . I was hoping to see her again."

"I see," Sara #11 nodded. "Is there anything more?"

Not being certain as to the proper response, I inquired, "Ma'am?"

Grimwald spoke next, "Ben, there are things happening that have given the Core a great deal of concern. Have you had any other interactions with Ruth?"

I managed to answer truthfully, "I have only seen her in my old bedchamber."

"Have you spoken to anyone else about Ruth?"

"I mentioned her name to George #111 . . . I lodge with him." To be sure, it was a half-truth, as I chose not to mention my discussions with Emmett.

"Okay," Sara #11 replied, appearing to be somewhat relieved.

Grimwald interjected, "There are things that Ruth may be involved in. We want you to come to us if you speak with her or if anyone else asks you about her. Do you understand?" The question was clearly a demand.

"Yes, sir."

Sara concluded the meeting. "Okay, thank you, Ben, you can go." She pointed in the direction of the doorway, prompting me to show no hesitancy in my departure.

To my dismay, as I hurriedly left her office, taking only two or three steps of my own, I ran directly into Emma #119 coming toward me. As we struck one another, her black-rimmed glasses were nearly displaced from her face. Clearly, she was not happy:

"Young man, remind me of your name?"

"Ben #239," I managed to reply.

"And just what are you doing out of class?" She removed her glasses, wiped them, and waited for my response.

"I was in Miss Sara's office, Ma'am."

She glanced toward the Governor-General's office door, "For what reason?"

"She asked to see me."

Emma put her glasses back in place, shook her head in dismay, and told me in no uncertain terms, "There is no running in these hallways. We have rules for a reason."

"Yes, Ma'am."

"I will be watching you, Ben #239. Understood?" She glared at me, shook her head once more, and then walked past to continue on her way in the direction of the "Personnel" doorway.

I turned quickly only to find myself standing before the "ATL Mission Office." Just inside the doorway was the young woman from the café. She smiled, "Sometimes Emma #119 can be a little harsh."

"Do you think?" I asked with a grin.

"I'm Athena #56," she said warmly. "I work for Milton #71."

She was far more attractive than I had realized, "My name is Ben #239."

"Nice to meet you, Ben #239."

Before we could speak further, we heard the voice of the Englishman calling from the inner office, "Athena, where did we put those upcoming assignments?"

"See you later," she said softly before turning and responding to his question, "I will show you."

I bid her farewell, returning to the classroom without further interaction.

As I sat at my desk, my mind repeatedly switched between thoughts of the Governor-General and Grimwald, Emma #119, and my brief (but altogether pleasant) conversation with Athena. It was only later, after Agnes had announced her usual "Class dismissed," that George and I had returned to our chamber, giving us occasion to speak. He was quick to ask: "What was the meeting all about?"

For a few moments, I sat in silence. I had debated with myself so frequently over the quandary of whether to tell him all that was occurring that I could take it no longer. I needed to be able to trust him. It seemed like the proper occasion was finally upon me.

"Can I have your complete confidence?"

"Absolutely," came his assurance.

"Let me show you my Horologium."

I removed the watch from my pocket and began by showing him the inscription within ("Help!R7"). I told him everything that I had come to know, expressing my desire to help Ruth #7 but admitting the confusion regarding just what was to be done. I described my conversations with Emmett and the matter of the ATL being changed. I also told him about the return trip to my own bedchamber at the time of my recruitment. The tale caused him some measure of surprise:

"That must have been amazing!"

I explained what I had learned about Elizabeth I, and the Francis Drake expedition that had changed the ATL. Such an excursion gave the appearance that England planned to colonize the New World ahead of schedule. I told him all that I had pondered about the situation. I described my meeting with the Governor-General, concluding with the concern I now held in mind, "I think Ruth may have discovered someone is influencing Elizabeth I and now finds herself in need of my assistance, or she may face eradication."

When I had completed my tale, George sat in silence for a long while, seemingly pondering all that I had related. He took a very long while to respond. The silence was maddening and my own impatience grew to the point where I was near to articulating something myself when he finally spoke:

"When I lived in London there was a popular saying that was often bandied about to describe the power of the English, 'The sun never sets on the British Empire.' Do you know what it means?"

"After my time, I am afraid."

"After George III lost the American Colonies, Britain began to colonize the world. There were countless excursions to all parts of the globe – territories that the British empire would eventually claim as its own. The saying meant that there was no place on earth in which the empire had not found a footing. I would have to examine the library to remember specific dates of some of the smaller countries and islands, but I do remember that England settled Australia in 1788, Canada in 1791, and India in 1858."

"What are you thinking?"

"Emmett told you that in order to control history, a time traveler only needed to choose someone with 'influence or authority?'"

"That's right," I agreed readily.

"And it appears that someone is Elizabeth I?"

"Yes," I quickly volunteered, not certain what my roomie had in mind.

"Perhaps it is not simply the American colonies we need to concern ourselves with. What if Elizabeth is being influenced to launch the British empire two hundred years ahead of schedule?"

"She could rule the world!"

George agreed. "Do you recall what Elder Professor Grimwald #94 told us the day we sat with him in the café?"

I shrugged my shoulders, uncertain as to what he meant.

"Don't you remember, he said that he had often had his own experiences with royalty? I believe he admitted that he had known quite a number of 'crowned heads?'"

I gasped in surprise, "It was Grimwald who told Sara that I was inquiring about Ruth #7!'

George nodded in the affirmative.

Your education will awaken the awareness that all time is one time. In the beginning, such may be hard to grasp but ultimately there is only NOW. Although its manifestations are infinite in scope, there is no time but NOW. Should you choose to hold in mind any perception other than this, know that it will be temporary at best – a diversion, giving you access to the illusion of any moment you might choose.

To be sure, you will possess the freedom to move about the Collective Illusion in any way you desire, giving yourself occasion to tour the enfoldment of history before you. As a Time Traveler, you may avail yourself of any moment imaginable, for all of history is within your grasp, and all those who have inhibited its illusion become accessible. In the beginning, such might appear to have meaning but ultimately you will come to understand its relevance no greater than a fallen leaf upon the wind.

Excerpt, "The Limitless Expression of Time," *A Time Traveler's Code of Conduct* **by Ruth #7**

SEVEN: *Journal Entry – April 17 ATL*

As I recall, it was a day or two after my interaction with Athena in the hallway, and not long after George and I arrived in the classroom that the League emergency buzzer began ringing throughout the entire facility. The incessant noise made any activity or conversation impossible, as the sound went on and on without interruption. While it continued, Agnes #23 moved about impatiently before us, waiting for it to stop. The delay caused her some measure of exasperation. When there was finally quiet and the bothersome blare had ceased, she gave voice to the "emergency assignment" that had just arrived from the ATL Mission Office.

"The alarm means we have no choice but to move quickly. Sometimes an issue must be addressed immediately!" she acknowledged nervously. "If we don't fix it now, it will create havoc on multiple timelines, making the assignment even harder to rectify." She took hold of the stylus, pointing at each of us in turn, "This is what happens when you are a time traveler. You do not get to choose the mission or decide when it is time to go to work." She turned to our French classmate and alerted her, "Bonne Souer Marie, this one is for you. You need to leave right away. You won't have the luxury of visiting the Akasha for information; I will give you a summation. Pay close attention!"

Agnes whipped around, taking occasion to write five words on the board, speaking each as they were underlined before us:

"Wild Snake Root = Milk Sickness."

"This was a serious problem!" Agnes assured us. "People died after drinking milk, and no one knew why. They called it 'Milk Sickness' – many families had two, three, or four deaths, and in some places, it wiped out whole communities. In a number of the American states, it was a problem for more than 100 years." Agnes #23 repeatedly tapped her stylus as she provided the insight which followed, "Do you know it was a Shawnee Indian woman who finally alerted settlers to the cause of all these deaths? Cows were eating the wild Snake Root plant and the plant was toxic to humans."

Our instructor turned to Bonne Souer Marie #304 and informed her, "Your skills with healing are needed immediately! The ATL Mission office has alerted us that the primary issue is within timeline XXXIII!"

Agnes moved excitedly about, adding for additional clarification. "I have been told that the problem is occurring on several timelines all at variance with the ATL but XXXIII is the most prominent. A twenty-two-year-old woman is dying in 1805 of Milk Sickness."

"Who is the woman?" Emanuel inquired.

"Her name is Nancy Hanks. Within a year she will marry, and within four she will have a daughter and a son." Our instructor was quick to add, "The approved timeline has her dying of Milk Sickness in 1818, not 1805. That is the problem!"

"What?" George reacted immediately. "Why does she have to die from Milk Sickness at all?"

Souer Marie quickly volunteered, "Madame, I can attend to both time periods? C'est possible."

Agnes stopped suddenly, refraining from any further movement. She stood firmly in place, speaking her words with unmistakable clarity: "A Wayfarer cannot deviate from the official mission. ATL history is not haphazard . . . it unfolds with a plan. There is always a plan, and the plan must be followed!"

George was not satisfied, "What could possibly be the reason?"

"There can be no departure from this assignment. Everything happens for a reason. This woman's death and her husband's remarriage will become defining points in the life of her son. He will learn from them, becoming who he is because of them."

Agnes motioned for our French student to come forward. "Bonne Souer Marie are you ready? You know what to do?"

Souer Marie nodded in the affirmative as she walked to the front of the classroom. As she stood next to Agnes, she took Horologium in hand and closed her eyes.

"Remember, you can only correct the problem in

1805. Do not interfere with 1818!"

Bonne Souer Marie mouthed the name "Nancy Hanks" repeatedly, moved to press the button, and a moment later she was gone, leaving Agnes alone at the front of the class.

"I still do not understand why she could not fix this completely," George stated aloud. "It does not feel right."

Agnes pointed her stylus and was adamant, "You cannot imagine how interference of this magnitude would create problems on countless timelines! The proper mission protocols are to be followed at all times."

George wanted to know more, "Who does she marry?"

"A young man named Thomas."

"And the name of the son?" came his final query.

Agnes sighed, clearly ready to move on with her curriculum, "He will be called 'Abraham.'" She tapped the stylus with some measure of irritation and waited for a moment before continuing, "The ATL has him scheduled to be president in 1861. Any other questions?"

When there were none, she declared, "Let us turn to the text. Manuela, please take notes for your roomie while she is away."

Upon Bonne Souer Marie's return, our French classmate was quick to inform us that her "emergency assignment" had been undertaken with complete adherence to mission guidelines. On this occasion, Nancy Hanks survived Milk Sickness, enabling all events within the ATL to remain in harmony with time travel protocols. To be sure, I do not believe that George #111 was completely satisfied with the outcome but the swiftness with which we moved on to our next assignments made revisiting the issue an indulgence for which we had little time.

I must admit, I was to receive quite a surprise when Agnes #23 stood before the class and read from the most recent "assignment list" just obtained from the ATL Mission Office:

"Emanuel #41, destination Nauvoo, Illinois, 1845, in the matter of the Latter-day Saints and their conflicting plans for westward migration."

"Manuela #64, destination Washington, DC, 1964, in the matter of Fannie Lou Hamer and the voting rights bill enforcing the Fifteenth Amendment."

"George #111, destination Dubai, United Arab Emirates, 2417, in the matter of Rashid Habib in her establishment of the Habib Foundation."

"Ben #239, destination Philadelphia, Pennsylvania, 1736, and the matter of alcohol, the Indians of the Six Nations, and James Logan . . ."

"What?" I interrupted, nearly jumping from my seat. For a time, I had once served as clerk on Logan's Pennsylvania Council.

Seemingly unhappy with the outburst, Agnes glared for a moment before completing the assignment list, "Bonne Souer Marie #304, destination Pusan, South Korea, 1950, in the matter of the first mobile Army surgical hospital."

Our instructress waved the mission list before us and advised with certainty, "I highly recommend a trip to the Akasha in order to gather the necessary information on these latest assignments. It is for that reason I am giving you the rest of the day off . . . I suggest you use your time wisely. Feel free to ask Emmett for help; he knows everything! Class dismissed."

As soon as we exited the classroom, George proved unable to contain his excitement, "I have never been to the future! Let me restate, I have never been to a future space-time illusion or a future NOW. This could be very exciting."

I agreed with his assessment before verbalizing my own thoughts, "As you are aware, I resided in Philadelphia. In fact, I was there in 1736." I added my misgiving, "There is something unusual about this assignment."

"What?"

I chose not to state that which was foremost in mind, adding only, "I am contemplating the matter but were the choice mine, I would have nothing to do with Philadelphia in 1736."

George shrugged once before returning to his own thoughts.

With new missions before us, the Akasha library became our joint destination. By this time I was well-acquainted with the journey, having traveled the various hallways and corridors on my own on multiple occasions. As such, the "officially approved League student handout" was no longer necessary as a map. We walked much of the way in silence. George was seemingly in contemplation of future wonders and I allowed my dreaded suspicion to move repeatedly through my mind. Aside from my skepticism about the newest assignment, I held some semblance of hope that I might find some brief occasion to speak with Emmett. When we came finally to the double doors, that thought was foremost in mind. Nonetheless, as much of the class would no doubt be researching the library at the very same time, my hope was not a certainty.

George and I laid claim to a table upon which to assemble whatever books became necessary in the matter of our research. He headed down one corridor and I journeyed in the opposite direction, looking for "background information" regarding our specific assignments. To be sure, I knew far more about Philadelphia in 1736 than George understood about Dubai in any time period. What remained unclear was the reliability of my suspicions about the ATL Mission Office sending me to Philadelphia in the first place. Could the reason I repeatedly contemplated truly be the primary rationale?

As I had some familiarity with the actual problem being portrayed as my present mission assignment, it was relatively easy to gather the remaining documents to ascertain what might best be done about the situation. I had known James Logan. He was president of the Pennsylvania Council and acting governor of the province. He was more than three decades my senior and well-established by the time I found occasion to serve as clerk in his assembly. We shared a love for Philadelphia and a love for books. A frequent champion of expanding the Pennsylvania colony, it was a cause that gave him regular interactions with the native Indian tribes.

From what I was able to discern from the records, the problem had originated due to a quarrel between a blacksmith, one Solomon Moffat, and an Indian by the name of Kaga, a member of the Six Nations. The two had apparently consumed a great deal of alcohol, aggravating whatever dispute arose between them. According to George Miranda, a trader who had witnessed the fight, the Indian had been the aggressor, as he had pulled a knife.

As is often the case in such matters of conflict, a far

different account was provided by others who witnessed the very same encounter. A tavern maiden and two Indians were present and described how Moffat had attacked first, repeatedly striking Kaga in the head. According to their report, Kaga had drawn the knife only in his own defense. In either event, the blacksmith struck a fatal blow and killed the Indian, before escaping the law and allegedly fleeing to the colony of Virginia.

The incident erupted anger and temperaments long-suppressed by both colonists and Natives alike. The Indians demanded justice; a number of the colonists wanted to be free of the "savage menace." On multiple timelines, this very issue had resulted in unruly violence from both sides and a number of deadly attacks on nearby Indian tribes by the colonists. This was the problem I had been asked to resolve.

During my library investigation, I endeavored to speak with Emmett, but as he was very much involved with Emanuel's background research, he had time only for a brief acknowledgment. As the situation with two British kings had adequately acquainted me with the records system within the Akasha, I was able to gather what materials I required for the assignment. When I became certain that I had all necessary information, I bid farewell to George, who remained busily involved in the acquisition of insights regarding Dubai, Rashid Habib, and matters of import that the twenty-fifth century had in store for him. I then took hold of the Horologium and proceeded to Philadelphia, choosing as my target James Logan, president of the provincial council.

As the method of these journeys has been examined on previous occasions, I will state only that after following the proper procedure and undergoing a fall of minimal duration, I arrived in Philadelphia. It came immediately to mind that the occasion would mark my second return. The previous excursion had taken place when I served as deathbed witness to myself as an old man. I knew, however, that a 1736 encounter with myself would entail observing a thirty-year-old man on the verge of his greatest sorrow.

I have noted how these matters of time travel diplomacy can be resolved by gathering some semblance of understanding amongst the various parties involved and discerning an arrangement to which all might find accord. This was to be the chosen approach for my present endeavor. To be sure, it became quickly apparent that although the issue of the two men (Moffat and Kaga) had given rise to the most recent discontent, it was not the sole problem. In the minds of James Logan, the seven remaining members of the Council, and the six Chiefs of the Indian Nations comprising the Native Confederacy, there were numerous concerns to be considered. There was the matter of ongoing encroachment into Indian territory. There was the belief that the white settlers received one level of justice while Indians received another. There was the issue of rum, brandy, and other strong liquor affecting the Indians – not only in the taverns but also being used by members of the council as a method of persuasion (encouraging Natives to become more accommodating to the demands of the council). The six Chiefs wanted their own people to be less inclined to the temptations of inns and tippling houses, as the problem of alcohol had been nonexistent prior to the arrival of colonists and European settlers. These were some of the questions before me.

In the end, it was simply a matter of influence and persuasion that gave life to a resolution addressing the most pressing problems. As all matters concerning the coexistence of settlers and the Indians could not be expected to become resolved in one document, it became apparent that the issues of alcohol and equal treatment were two in which the council and the chiefs could readily concur. After repeated usage of my Horologium, and assisting Logan, several of the Chiefs and two members of the Council to give voice to a harmonious outcome, all parties agreed that a warrant for the arrest of one Solomon Moffat would be issued and that the council would assist the Indian Confederacy in their desire to thereafter encourage abstinence from alcohol. The following proclamation was issued and signed by James Logan, given to the six Chiefs, and communicated throughout the entire colony:

"It has been agreed between us that we should suffer no injury to be done to one of your people more than to our own, nor without punishing the offender in the same manner as if it had been done to one of our people. Wherefore this council issues a warrant for the arrest of one Solomon Moffat, whose presumed whereabouts is in the colony of Virginia."

"This order also institutes an act against selling rum and other strong liquors to the Indians. All persons whatsoever are by said act prohibited directly or indirectly to sell, barter, give, or exchange, by themselves or others, any rum, brandy, or other strong liquors to any Indian within this province, under the penalty of their forfeiting ten pounds."

Once the document had been signed, such became law, resolving both the problem at hand and rectifying the issue within the approved timeline. With such matters settled, I next directed my attention to the primary reason I believed the ATL Mission Office had afforded the assignment to me in the first place. I was convinced beyond any doubt whatsoever that the principal purpose for my journey to Philadelphia in 1736 was not about a conflict between Indians and colonists but instead concerned nothing less than the death of a four-year-old.

I took the Horologium in hand, tapped its hands to stay within the selfsame year, gave thought to the seriousness of the issue I was about to face, stated my own name, pressed "TEMPUS," and breathed.

Only a parent who has undergone the loss of a child can fathom the magnitude of such a happening on the rest of one's life. Nary a day has passed that I have not given thought to my son, Franky, and cherished his memory within my heart and mind. He was only four when he died, and though more than fifty years have passed, I still remember how it felt to lift him into my arms, how it felt to run my fingers through the curls of his brown hair, and how it felt to kiss the softness of his cheek at night. He was a very special child.

It is perhaps a certainty that every mother or father will consider their offspring to be quite extraordinary but Franky, indeed, was golden. The light he put forth with his smile was witnessed by all those who came to be near him. He had the brightest eyes and the cleverest mind of any child in the colonies. He was beautiful and healthy, and ever so willing to learn more about the world around him. He was the delight of our home and all who met him. He was a joy. He was ever so curious. He was our everything. When he was gone, our lives would never be the same.

Even now, the sorrow about his departure is extremely hard for me to be put into words. There is both great sadness and abundant measures of regret. I have missed him every day, and the knowledge of my own involvement in the matter of his passing has given way to guilt and hopelessness and anguish so deep I have chosen not to speak of it, until now. Franky died of smallpox, and he died only because I had not championed his inoculation, whereas I had promptly attended to the matter of my own. How might a father turn loose of such remorse?

To be sure, my wife, Deborah, was not in favor of such measures, but I cannot and must not lay the blame solely before her. She was not alone in such misgivings. In fact, these doubts and uncertainties were common throughout the colonies. Countless voices remained adamant that inoculation was untested. The act of creating an incision in one's own body and placing live pus from another's infection into such an opening was seen as folklore, if not an outright crime. Such a practice brought forth heated debates and angry outbursts from those who knew no better. Repeated articles about the issue had certainly appeared within the papers but only a few championed inoculation. A majority favored a cautionary approach until medicine could more thoroughly approve such methodology. Those less educated argued that inoculations were "Devil's work," violating the very will of God; if the Divine chose to call you to your Heavenly home, inoculations were nothing less than opposition to one's Maker. These were the voices that had swayed Deborah. I could have countered my wife in the necessity of Franky's inoculation. I should have. I ought to have taken the entire question into my own hands but I did not. I failed miserably in attending to the health of my son, and I have suffered immeasurably because of it. I shall never forgive myself.

I was certain that this happening had been the sole

issue giving rise to the occasion of an "assignment" in Philadelphia. Whether it was a task from the Core, the ATL Mission Office, or the League itself, I knew not but the matter before me was truly the reason I had been appointed a return.

Although the room had been darkened in an effort to lessen the light coming into his room (and the pain that came to the boy, as the light hurt his eyes), I could see the vaporous form of my time-traveling self. It moved about the figure of the man I had once been in waves of motion like a bedcovering floating gently in the breeze. My wife sat in the corner of the room, sobbing with her head between her hands. The figure of myself stared in hopelessness at the child who was slipping away. My younger self used the palm of his hand to occasionally brush the side of Franky's head. My boy's face and arms were covered with the very blisters that gave indication of the malaise he suffered. My child's only sound an occasional and soft groan as if the remaining air itself was being forced from his lungs. He was feverish to the touch. He no longer opened his eyes. The mind of the man I had once been knew the time was near. I gave thought to my former self that he should place a final kiss on the cheek of my son so that I could feel the skin of my child's face against my own lips.

How could such a tragedy be allowed in the mind of Creation? How could a father's one neglect cause such devastation for the remainder of one's life? How could this foremost tragedy that Deborah and I shared be the one subject we could never discuss between us? How could the heartbreak we had shared become the very thing that pushed us apart?

As I observed the scene before me and allowed such thoughts of sadness to race through my mind, I knew I had the power to change it. It would be simple enough.

I could go back six months before the scene I witnessed and strengthen my former self's resolve in the matter of Franky's inoculation. I could lessen Deborah's opposition, as well. I could alter what became the path of our marriage from this point forward. I could champion the cause of these inoculations and save so many more from unnecessary grief. I could save myself from a lifetime of heartache and pain, setting aside every measure of remorse and guilt and despair. All these things could be accomplished simply by saving the life of my four-year-old.

As these thoughts crossed my mind, I stood wondering what harm would come to clutch the Horologium and make such a simple change upon the timeline. I revisited the idea again and again, as I heard my wife sobbing and saw the tears of the man I had once been fall to the bedcovering below. I allowed my ghostly fingers to wipe my own eyes as I stood there, coming ever so close to taking hold of the timepiece. All I had to do was to use the watch. Just use the watch. It would be so easy to set things right. I came ever so close to doing just that but in the end, I knew I could not. I knew I must not.

When I could bear the scene before me no longer, I took one final look at my son, wiped my eyes, took the Horologium in hand, and returned to the library from whence I had come.

Upon my arrival, Milton #71 was there waiting for me. He said straight away, "You passed." He stood next to the table where I had piled my background information of books, nodding approvingly as he patted me once on the shoulder. "Congratulations, you passed the examination."

"It is not a test I would choose to take again," I replied softly.

"It is most regrettable, Chap," Milton appeared sincere, "but we must test a Wayfarer's resolve in this issue of not manipulating one's personal timeline. I trust you will keep this matter to yourself until your classmates have undergone their own assessment, as well?"

"I will."

"Very good," Milton responded before adding, "Are you going to be okay?"

I repeated, "I will."

He turned to go and then stopped to add further to the conversation, "By the way, Athena asked me to suggest that the two of you might have lunch sometime – if you are agreeable?"

Had the invitation come before my return to Philadelphia, I would have jumped with enthusiasm. In my present frame of mind, I was able to say only, "That would be nice."

"I will let her know." He then turned to leave.

I had some semblance of personal exhaustion but remained unclear as to whether the fatigue was most due to the journey or because of the scene I had just witnessed. As I gathered my thoughts, I saw Manuela wave. I acknowledged her presence before her own departure. Afterward, I turned to put in order the books that I had removed from the library shelves – a project which was nearing completion when Emmett walked to my side.

"Was it a success?" he asked.

"I believe so."

He looked around to ascertain whether we were alone and could speak freely. "I am sorry we could not talk earlier."

I said assuredly, "It is not a problem." Although I knew there were several things I had wished to convey to him, each had completely faded from my mind.

Emmett looked about once more before relating what was uppermost in his thoughts, "You need to know that two members of the Core have been exploring the historical records for themselves – records that relate to a specific time period."

"What time period?"

The old man appeared uneasy, "Elizabethan England."

"Which members of the Core?"

"Grimwald #94 and Emma #119," were the names that fell from his lips.

It is all too inevitable that occasions will arise when you find the ultimate goal of our Work to appear far beyond your reach. The ongoing nature of our tasks, the never-ending enumeration of "things that may still be" enduring ever out of accord with the ATL, and holding the understanding in mind that in spite of every accomplishment undertaken thus far your goal will appear just as distant as before. These things will take their toll upon every time traveler.

When such occurs, however, know that there is ever growth and there is ever movement forward, and with every mission success the League moves closer than ever before to the goal we have chosen to accomplish. Be not faint of heart.

Excerpt, "The Prime Directive," *A Time Traveler's* **Code of Conduct by Ruth #7**

EIGHT: Journal Entry – April 20 ATL

"This story is simply amazing!" Agnes #23 declared with her usual enthusiasm. "It is certainly one of my favorite case histories!" With stylus in hand, she wrote the name "Sir Victor Goddard" on the whiteboard before us, underlined, and proceeded with the tale:

"Goddard became famous for saving the British forces at Dunkirk in 1940!" She stated with admiration, "It was actually his idea to send the armada of small boats to rescue the entire army! But it was his experience out of time five years earlier that would influence him for the rest of his life." Agnes shook her head in disgust and pointed her stylus at no one in particular, "Unfortunately, most of those hindered by space-time have completely forgotten his involvement at Dunkirk, and almost no one gave thought to his time slip. You know, all this ignorance makes our job so much harder."

Our instructress bobbed about while speaking, "Goddard was an Air Marshal for the British Royal Air Force. In 1935, he was flying his biplane . . ." she paused and quickly held up two fingers before us, "that means there were two sets of wings. He was flying from the base in Edinburgh, Scotland to his home airfield in Andover, England. Not far from Edinburgh, there was an abandoned airfield in a small village by the name of Drem. It had been deserted after the Great War. Obviously, no one called it World War I until the later conflict."

She turned to write the name "Drem" on the board, underlining it twice, just as my roomie turned to me, smiled, and silently mouthed the words: "Background information."

Agnes continued, "As he was flying over the old airfield, he made note of its condition. The airstrip was overgrown with shrubbery. The few hangars and buildings still standing were dilapidated. There were cows grazing all over the area. In terms of its former standing as an airbase, Drem was in complete shambles."

The stylus resumed its movement before us, "Goddard continued flying his plane toward Andover when all at once he flew into a storm. He was surrounded by clouds, which made visual flight impossible. High winds tossed his plane about. Goddard lost control and the plane started spiraling to the ground. Goddard was worried. Using all of his strength, he was finally able to pull back on the control stick and the plane leveled off. When he looked down at the ground to find his bearings, he discovered he had been turned around and the plane was heading back to Drem. Only this time, things looked very different than they had appeared just a few moments before."

She nodded with satisfaction, "The storm was gone. Goddard and his plane were flying in brilliant sunlight. All of his surroundings were clear. He was astonished to see that the abandoned airfield was now bustling with activity! The airfield was pristine. The hangars were all new. Although he saw a few familiar biplanes like his own, he also saw something that the Royal Airforce did not possess in 1935 – the ground was covered with yellow monoplanes!" Agnes #23 held up her forefinger and clarified, "That means ONE wing!"

"The entire airfield was busy with pilots and mechanics running around, and to Goddard's surprise, the mechanics wore blue overalls . . . something he had never seen before." Agnes caused her hand and the stylus to fly before our eyes and then circle around, going back in the other direction, "Goddard turned the plane around in the direction of Andover, only this time when he looked down the Drem airfield was once more in ruins."

Our instructress paused, allowing us to grasp the importance of the tale. "When World War II finally occurred, everything Goddard had seen at Drem came to pass. It is just an amazing story. Amazing! And Goddard chose to tell it for the rest of his life. Even with his military standing and his spotless reputation, he was not afraid to discuss the paranormal."

Our teacher lowered her stylus to her desk, exchanging it for an old newspaper she had lying in place. "This is Sir Victor Goddard's obituary dated January 27, 1987." She began reading:

"Goddard experienced possibly the most famous 'slip through time' ever recorded when in 1935 he flew over the near-derelict site of the Drem Airfield in Scotland in a heavy storm. He suddenly saw in bright sunlight a meticulously accurate vision of the airfield as it was to be four or five years later, with the yellow monoplanes which had not yet been designed being wheeled out by mechanics in the blue overalls which had not yet been adopted . . ." She stopped reading and looked up at her students.

"It is right here in black and white," she said with certainty, "and yet most people remain totally unaware of this story."

George and I finally found occasion to provide one another with details of our most recent mission assignments. We chose to stay up late in order to share our respective experiences. To be sure, the details of my return to Philadelphia focused only upon James Logan, the Pennsylvania Council, the Chiefs of the Six Nations, and the issue between one Solomon Moffat and the Indian, Kaga. I confess to giving no mention to either Franky or the pain of revisiting the occasion of my greatest sorrow. Although such had been the promise I had made to Milton #71 upon my return, I also knew that I could not speak of such things and hope to retain any measure of composure.

My roomie reminded me that he had visited Philadelphia during the course of his life (his dry goods firm even possessed a location within the very city) but after my discussion, he soon made it clear that the city he had come to know was far different than my own. By his own account, Philadelphia had nearly tripled in size and ongoing relations with the Indians had become a thing of the past, for the natives had migrated far from the surrounding areas.

I explained the resolution I had helped influence, resulting in Moffat's warrant and the consequential fine for the purchase of alcohol by any member of the tribes. It was made clear how such measures provided a resolution for all involved and addressed the various problems within multiple timelines. At no time during my assessment of the mission, however, did a matter prove difficult for George to understand or were words utilized beyond my listener's comprehension. Such was not my experience when my roomie detailed his own adventure.

George recounted how the Dubai he had occasion to visit was much more agreeable than the hot desert climate of its past, due to weather control, a subject which I shall attempt to detail momentarily. The city was cosmopolitan, consisting of people from all backgrounds, faiths, and experiences. In such a place, one Rashid Habib oversaw a "conglomerate" (this is the very word used by my roomie) with business dealings in communication, energy storage, and medical technologies. His task was to assist said Rashid Habib in creating a foundation that would underwrite both research and human endeavor for the foreseeable future, if not in perpetuity.

Such an assignment was easy enough to understand. The complications arose as George described the world of the twenty-fifth century and how things had changed. Accordingly, I have chosen to note here only those portions of the tale for which I possessed any semblance of understanding. With such in mind, I will summarize my comprehension of the world that George described from his visit thusly: the people are numerous but their numbers are stable, the weather is a matter of choice and design, and the food is very much different than anything you might choose to imagine.

In George's own words, "The Akasha library provides a record that in 1800 the global population was approximately one billion people. By 2400 that figure has surpassed 10 billion but it is relatively stable, as the annual births and deaths are near equal to one another." He eyed me closely, "I can tell you that with the exception of a few historical sites, there is no such thing as a cemetery. There is no longer room for such sentimentality."

I found myself intrigued, "What do they do with the bodies of those who are deceased?"

"Recycling and laser-induced disintegration," came his reply.

"Explain so that the matter is more understandable to me."

"Whatever can be reused is reused; the remainder becomes vaporized into nothingness by an energetic beam of light."

Although his response provided almost no additional clarity, I responded nonetheless, "I see."

"While I was there, I also learned that they have designed the most amazing approach for controlling the weather."

"What?" Although his words were quite clear to me, the concept seemed far beyond any rational understanding.

My roomie nodded in the affirmative, "Yes, it is all very much planned in advance. They have learned how to control the weather."

I found myself dumbfounded, "In a city?"

"No, of the entire planet."

"How is such even possible? Explain."

"There are satellites . . ." was all he could state before the confusion upon my face caused him to begin anew, "there are machines in the sky – far above the earth – that create a global energetic web . . . like a big net. This net controls everything within the atmosphere: the rain, the snow, the heat, the cold, the wind. The weather is regulated for the benefit of all people and places and crops."

"It is difficult to fathom," I admitted freely. "How do these machines get into the sky?"

"They create themselves with multi-dimensional space printers and robotics and all manner of technology," he said matter-of-factly.

"That is entirely unclear to me, as well, but perhaps it is best that we simply continue."

"They have created the technology to print objects in the sky."

"No need to understand," I shook my hand before him. "What else did you find of interest?"

"The food is very different than what you may imagine, as well."

I eyed him cautiously, "Tell me."

My roomie appeared very much amused as he sounded off the items while counting upon his fingertips: "I made note of seaweed, manufactured fish and meat . . ."

"What?" I interrupted.

"They have discovered how to grow fish and meat from itself."

"What?" I repeated.

"They can take a tiny portion of any meat or fish and cause it to replicate itself. They farm algae and grains and jellyfish and create every manner of plant-based protein and produce. They also harvest insects for protein."

Certainly, I had misgivings and doubts about such

fare, "I think I would prefer boiled potatoes and turkey."

"You can have turkey but it doesn't come from a farm. It comes from a lab."

I responded, "I see," as the matter was vaguely clear to me, yet it was a very long while indeed before I could eliminate thoughts of such morsels from my mind.

"When did you start working for Milton #71?" I asked Athena #56. The two of us sat across from one another at a small table in the League café. I couldn't help but be drawn to the intensity of her brown eyes.

She smiled, "I have always been good at history and keeping records. When I first arrived, I really thought I might end up working with Emmett but he likes to do his own thing. The ATL Mission Office was a good fit, so I have been there for a while."

I liked her. It was not just her beauty or her voice or the way her eyes stared intensely back at me when I spoke, I found myself interested in her. Indeed, this felt very different than what I remembered from the passions of my youth.

"What's it like working in the mission office?"

"Well, it is interesting." She smiled again (I smiled in return), and she added, "I think I like the research the best. History is fascinating and watching how easily timelines can be changed by the actions of one person or one event never gets boring."

I noticed how Athena took the hair behind her ear, curling it around her fingertip as she spoke. I was glad that my roomie, George, had declined to join us for lunch.

I had invited him but he had been quick to respond, "I think your girlfriend wants to be alone with you."

"Do you ever get to time travel?" I asked.

Athena nodded, "Of course." She turned loose of her hair, reached inside a pocket, and showed me her Horologium. "Mostly it's background assignments but I think they are just as fascinating as timeline missions."

"Did you have Agnes #23 as your teacher when you got here?"

"Oh yes," she smiled, "Agnes and her curriculum . . . a little annoying but very interesting. I think my favorite case histories were the Moberly-Jourdain time slip and the Medieval time slip."

"We've talked about Moberly-Jourdain – the French teachers. Haven't heard the Medieval story yet."

"Don't worry, you will."

I really liked her. I gave thought to the idea of reaching across the table and taking her hand into my own but decided against it. Was it too soon? It had been a long while since I had involved myself in such matters. I queried, "I guess knowing history is essential for what you do?"

"Well, it is my background but Milton is the real historian. He is the primary historian on the Core. That's perfect for his job with mission oversight."

She lowered her voice, "I probably shouldn't tell you this but Milton always lets me know what's happening around here. I really like working with him. Apparently, some members of the Core have called a special meeting . . . more of a hearing really. I guess a few of them think Ruth #7 has been altering the ATL."

"Why do they think that?"

"Well, Milton doesn't believe it but apparently there is proof," she said softly.

"What kind of proof?"

"I don't know if you know this but every time you influence a timeline, your Horologium leaves a mark upon the ATL record – a kind of signature."

"You can tell where we've been?"

"Only when you influence a timeline," she smiled, "but remember there are so many possibilities within each timeline, it only comes to our attention if it is out of accord with the ATL, or if someone is specifically looking for it. Apparently, somebody looked into Ruth's timeline travels and became suspicious."

I pulled the timepiece out of my pocket and held it before her, "How does the recording work?"

"It's linked to your identity," she said simply. "Turn your watch over."

I turned over the Horologium and she pointed to my name inscribed on the back cover, "See, Ben #239. If you only journey for a background mission that's not recorded because there is no impact upon the timeline. Whenever you influence someone or something in history, it is uploaded to the Akasha. That is how the record is made – changes to the timeline."

I considered her statement for several moments before confessing a youthful transgression, "When I was a child, I penned a number of letters using a name that was not my own. I hoped to convince others I was someone I was not. Could that be done with a Horologium?"

"You mean like identity fraud?" She looked confused and twirled a strand of her hair between her fingertips as she contemplated the matter. After a moment, she shook her head and admitted, "I don't know."

I sought further clarification, "If the Core makes changes to the approved timeline, how do you know?"

"If it is part of the ATL, there is no reason to investigate. The ATL Mission Office is only responsible for things out of alignment with the approved timeline."

"What will happen to Ruth?"

"Well, I guess the Core could recommend either probation or expulsion. I can't believe that Ruth would actually do any of this. Honestly, I don't know what's going to happen. I don't think Milton knows either. He told me there's some dissension within the Core: jealousy, disagreement, normal people stuff." Athena lowered her voice to a whisper, "If the approved timeline really is being changed, that sounds more like Emma to me."

"Why Emma?"

"Haven't you ever noticed how the people most concerned with the rules are usually the first ones to actually break them?"

Before I had a chance to respond, the school bell went off, announcing the end of the lunch break.

"I have to go back to work," Athena replied.

I responded quickly without thinking, "When can we have another date?"

"Was this a date?" she smiled.

As has often been the case with these verbal class reports, I found Emanuel's discussion of the Latter-day Saints (or Mormons as I learned they are called) and the challenges of their relocation to be of great interest. I prefer here to set aside any thoughts I might have on the subject of religion in general and some of their founder's (Joseph Smith's) claims in particular, choosing instead to focus upon the question of persecution, their desire for freedom of worship, the matter of their westward migration, and how their various factions created problems within the ATL.

Emanuel stood before us and briefly reflected upon the religion's beginnings – matters, to be sure, that those who have interest may discover for themselves. Our Swede classmate was thoroughly informed on the topic (and Agnes appeared quite focused on the taking of notes) as he went on to describe how on multiple occasions the Mormon faithful had been forced to move from one place to another, being driven from their homes by those who were less than tolerant. Emanuel told the class, "They journeyed from New York to Ohio to Missouri, and finally to Nauvoo, Illinois, which they hoped would become their final home. It was not."

I came to consider this fact from his account one of great irony from two perspectives. In the first, many of the New England colonies had been settled by men and women who themselves had departed Europe in an effort to escape their own religious persecution, and it would be the very descendants of these immigrants who chose to hold prejudice against the Mormons in return. Of second import is that from Emanuel's description the Mormons seemed to be less than tolerant of other faiths, believing their own to be the one true Church. Whether this belief caused them to seek only the company of their own kind, or whether it was persecution that prompted them to seek separation, I know not but they sought to find refuge and isolation from all others.

Emanuel described their issue of primary concern, as follows: "Even after a few years, the Mormons found that Nauvoo was truly no better than any of their previous homes. Joseph Smith had long been persecuted for his beliefs and his practice of polygamy. In time, he would be killed by an angry mob. The event caused a crisis in his own succession, as well as a crisis in this matter of their migration. Smith had been considering several destinations for the faithful but the matter of where they were going had not been fully resolved at the time of his death."

"This issue became a problem on several timelines," Emanuel explained. "Joseph Smith had considered locations in Canada, California, Utah, and Texas. Excluding Canada, the proponents of each of the others became major forces in their own right and nearly pulled the church apart with dissension. My assignment was to fix this problem created by strong wills and opposing perspectives along timelines XI, XL, and LXXVI."

"Let's start with Texas," Emanuel reflected aloud. "For a time, Texas had been Smith's favored location. This destination was under the charge of one Lyman Wight, who led a Mormon delegation of 200 followers to the territory. Wight had even been appointed one of the Church's Twelve Apostles by Joseph Smith himself and the plan for Texas was nothing less than brilliant."

Emanuel #41 wrote the word "Texas" on the board, causing Agnes to nod with satisfaction while making a notation.

"At the time, ownership of the enormous territory from the southernmost portion of Texas to the Pacific Ocean was in dispute. Both Texas and Mexico laid claim to the area. Wight was charged with buying the land from Texas (regardless of whether or not they actually owned it) and offering the Texans help in defending their borders from the Mexican Army. The Mormons would amass an army of their own, the territory would be claimed as the independent country of Deseret, and the area would become the center for all Latter-day Saints."

"Not only was this a problem for the ATL on numerous

perspectives," Emanuel added for our benefit, "but it
started to create major changes to additional timelines
dealing with United States history and its future."

"You probably don't need to hear all of the details but
this was fixed by encouraging President John Tyler to
annex the disputed areas for the United States during his
final days as president, which absolutely undermined
the Mormon plan for an independent country. I also
used the Horologium and reminded Lyman Wight of
the rift that already existed between himself and the
rest of the church hierarchy. You see, Wight was never
in full agreement with the church's choice of Brigham
Young as Smith's successor. Wight was also adamant
that Texas had always been the preferred location for
the faithful – after all, it had been Joseph Smith's idea
from the start. With this as his motivation, he decided
to establish the church himself in Texas, regardless of
how the Mormon hierarchy had changed its plans. For
this act, he was eventually excommunicated. When that
happened, the timeline problem for Texas ceased to
exist. Wight's contingency of Mormons became known
as the Reorganized Church of Latter-day Saints and
eventually the Community of Christ – an offshoot of the
original faith."

Emanuel turned back to the board and wrote
"California," while Agnes made her notation. He
continued, "It had long been the desire of the faithful to
head westward to the coast. One route was the journey
undertaken by Brigham Young, who led 148 pioneers
from Illinois to Nebraska and then Wyoming, traveling
westward along the Oregon Trail. The journey was
almost 1,300-miles and due to poor weather and frequent
stops, it took 17 months to accomplish. The other route
was appointed to Samuel Brannan, a church leader, who
recruited 70 men, 68 women, and their 100 children to

sail from New York Harbor to the southernmost point of South America around Cape Horn, then northward to Hawaii and then east to the California coast – a distance covering 24,000 miles and taking nearly six months. They came ashore at the port city of Yerba Buena, which would come to be called San Francisco."

"The problem here was that Brannan's group was so strong that it threatened to split the faithful between California and those who had journeyed to Utah. In fact, the Mormon settlement in California soon tripled the population of the surrounding areas."

Emanuel wrote the final destination, "Utah," on the board, "Utah had not been the original destination. Early on, Mormon leadership had desired to migrate to the West Coast. It was only after Brigham Young received favorable reports on the Salt Lake basin combined with the fact that his pioneers had already been exhausted by their 1,300-mile trek that Utah was chosen as 'the place.' Once Brigham Young's group had settled in Utah, Brannan traveled east to meet with Young and tried to convince him to bring the pioneers to California, as had been the original plan. Young disagreed and rejected the idea. Brannan returned to California very much frustrated, and that frustration created further dissension and a problem within the timeline."

"I had to fix this, as well." Emanuel sounded determined. "During my time with Brannan, it became clear that even more important to him than the Church was his love of land and property. Once he was settled in San Francisco and had opened a trading store, he started buying real estate. In addition to the money from the store, as church leader in California, he was still collecting tithes from the Mormon faithful who had accompanied him. His frustration with Young caused him to withhold these funds from the church headquarters in Utah. It was a simple matter really to encourage Brannan (who was not at all opposed to the idea) to use church funds to purchase additional property. In time, he had holdings from San Francisco to Sacramento and beyond. He became one of California's wealthiest citizens. Because he had withheld money from the Church, he was eventually discharged from his position in the hierarchy, causing many of the faithful who had followed him in the first place to change their allegiance and travel instead to Utah."

Emanuel concluded by saying, "With the problems of Texas and California resolved, Utah became the favored destination within the ATL and all problems were resolved. This is how I fulfilled my most recent mission assignment."

When he finished, everyone applauded for the information provided (if not for the fact that his lengthy discussion had, at last, come to an end), and my roomie queried with enthusiasm, "Should we all go to the café?"

Although I had readily agreed with the suggestion, as I walked down the hallway I could not help but consider how easily a work of any nature might be undermined by those who were a part of it – whether it be in the matters of a church or in the activities of a League pursuing the rectification of timelines.

It is a certainty that occasions will arise when a mission needs to be revisited. Even the most skillful Wayfarer provided with every manner of insight and information from the Akasha may commit errors in judgment. There will also be unforeseen obstacles or issues of complication arising from conflicting timelines. Furthermore, a time traveler must ever hold in mind an understanding that the dynamic of free will possessed by every target of influence cannot be underestimated.

Do not let these complications sway you from the task, for each of these things can be rectified. Every problem can be reevaluated and every moment within the illusion of space-time can be readdressed. Such remains the opportunity ever before you.

Excerpt, "Revisiting Your Timeline Assignment," *A Time Traveler's Code of Conduct* **by Ruth #7**

NINE: *Journal Entry – April 22 ATL*

I realize thus far I have neglected to detail the journeyman Wayfarer's visit to our class one afternoon, providing us with a "surprise special guest appearance," as Agnes #23 chose to describe the occasion. Quite apart from our teacher's apparent disinterest during the previous guest presentation entailing two speakers from the Core (and their rousing discourse on the "League Disciplinary Process"), for this event, our instructress was truly enthusiastic. She stood at the front of the classroom next to a woman of seeming Middle Eastern descent while exclaiming with much excitement:

"This is Nashwa #86. We were in class together back in the old days. It is so wonderful that she's able to join us today!" She bounced about with such spirited vigor that Nashwa was forced to take a step sideways as a means of preventing the two women from colliding one with another.

Agnes continued her introduction, "Nashwa is one of the League's time travelers. She works for us out on the 'front lines' – out in the field!" She eyed us somberly. "I have asked her to come and answer any questions you might have about being a Wayfarer. Please welcome our guest." Agnes clapped her hands wholeheartedly and continued with such clapping until we were left with little choice but to join her. When the applause finally seemed sufficient enough, she took a seat of her own.

Nashwa #86 nodded in appreciation, "Thanks for inviting me. Your instructor and I have been friends for a very long time, so I am delighted she asked me to come here today and answer any questions you might have about this work. Let me start by confirming, yes, I am a time traveler and yes, I enjoy my job."

"And she does it so well," Agnes interrupted from where she sat.

Nashwa replied, "Thank you, Agnes," and then queried, "Who has the first question?"

Manuela #64 quickly raised her hand. Our guest speaker pointed in her direction while stating, "Tell me your name and your question."

"My name is Manuela #64. What do you like best about being a Wayfarer?"

"Umhhh," Nashwa appeared to consider the matter. "Most of all, I think I enjoy helping the League with its work. I consider myself honored to participate in such an incredible endeavor. Secondly, it has been a wonderful experience being part of such an amazing community of people who share similar thoughts and ideas about the work we are doing."

"And what do you like least?" Manuela inquired.

"I have to admit that when you are alone, by yourself, somewhere in the Collective Illusion, it can be quite lonely sometimes. Obviously, that is why some Wayfarers choose to work here at headquarters. While you are here, you always have others nearby."

Emanuel waved his hand about, drawing attention to himself so that he might next have a turn. Nashwa pointed in his direction.

"I have heard that we will get to manage our appearance . . ." he said.

"Name?" our guest interrupted.

"Emanuel," he replied and quickly asked again, "I have heard that we will get to manage our appearance at some point. When does that happen?"

"When you are a journeyman Wayfarer, Milton #71 and the ATL Mission Office will work with you on that. The office will help you make those decisions. I believe you can also make changes from time to time, if you desire."

My roomie went next. "My name is George #111," he said without being called upon. "What kind of mission assignments do you get?"

"Everything you can imagine," came her first reply. "The ATL Mission Office will come to know where to send you and how to best use your talents, whether it's a specific type of problem or a certain time period. Every Wayfarer gets their assignments from the mission office. Personally, I have a fondness for all matters dealing with Russia or the Ottoman Empire but I have been a part of many, many missions throughout history."

Bonne Soeur Marie #304 was called upon next, "You can call me Marie #304," she said. "Where do you go when you don't have a specific assignment?"

"Generally, you can find me on a beach in some place

or time. On occasion, I come here to see old friends." She smiled at Agnes.

Emanuel chose to ask a second question, "Who taught you and Agnes #23 when you were both in school?"

"Elder Professor Grimwald #94 was our regular instructor, but back then the curriculum was often shared by another teacher." Nashwa glanced back at our instructress as though there was more to the tale but said only, "Agnes has mastered the curriculum better than anyone else."

I chose to go next, "Ben #239," and then asked, "Who was the other instructor?"

Nashwa #86 paused momentarily before responding, "We had several guest speakers during our coursework but Grimwald often shared the curriculum with Bruce #29."

"And where is he now?" I inquired.

Nashwa was quick to respond, "He is no longer with us."

George repeated my query, "Where is he?"

Nashwa appeared noticeably nervous as she looked toward our instructress, seeking some manner of assistance.

Agnes #23 replied from her seat, voicing some measure of frustration, "He is no longer a part of the school!"

Bonne Soeur Marie questioned, as well, "Pourquoi? Why?"

Our guest speaker finally relented, "He had been making changes to his own timeline – small at first and then with greater regularity. He was finally caught when those changes began affecting the ATL. He was a good teacher but the Core really had no choice in the matter."

Manuela #64 put her hand in the air while inquiring,

"How come he wasn't caught right away?"

"Good question," came Nashwa's response. "There are many choices we can all make that don't necessarily impact the greater timeline – choosing what you eat for breakfast is a good example. It is only when an individual makes changes causing a ripple in the timeline that the ATL is truly affected."

I put my hand in the air but did not wait to be called upon, "Was Bruce #29 eradicated or simply dismissed?"

Nashwa appeared uneasy, "I am not certain how to answer that."

Agnes #23 yelled from her seat, "He would have been eradicated if he hadn't gotten away!"

I took my class text in hand and turned toward the back of the book. The occasion seemed ideal to seek clarity regarding a statement we had covered earlier in class: "Regarding this issue of capture and eradication, I have a question about the League Disciplinary Process. Let me read it here: 'Upon approval of the Governor-General anyone suspected of a serious violation of time travel protocols may be tracked at any time without their knowledge or consent.' What does that mean?"

For the second time, our instructor yelled from her seat, saying only, "The Governor-General's Horologium has the ability!"

My follow-up questions came next, "Does this matter of one's removal from the League occur with any regularity? And how frequently does this matter of escaping from the Core take place?"

Nashwa appeared somewhat perplexed before responding, "I am not generally here at League headquarters. Agnes, do you know the answer to these questions?"

Agnes was frustrated as she stood to respond to my queries, "These things are matters of Core business!"

She eyed me seriously, "I would take such questions to Miss Sara if I were you. However, I have known of several instances where a Wayfarer got away before a decision regarding eradication could be enacted."

"What happens to these Wayfarers who escape from the League?" I could not help but inquire.

Agnes responded before Nashwa had the chance but she was obviously not happy, "There are members of the League who work full-time tracking down these dissidents!" She added quickly, "Does anyone else have a *real* question about being a Wayfarer?"

My roomie responded to her call, "What was your favorite assignment, Nashwa #86?"

Nashwa then chose to recount a most interesting tale of her influence upon one Princess Sophie of Poland who journeyed to Russia for marriage, overthrew her own husband, and came to be called Catherine the Great.

I should note that I chose to arise early the next day, making my way to the Akasha library before the morning class. As I had finally recovered from the interlude within my own past, I wished to tell Emmett of my meeting with the Governor-General and alert him to my own unease that Elder Professor Grimwald appeared to be at least an informant of some kind in the Ruth situation, if not personally involved. The fact that Grimwald #94 and Emma #119 had been exploring the records on Elizabethan England also gave me cause for concern. I found myself hopeful that Emmett had acquired at least some additional information on the two.

To my dismay, when I arrived at the massive double doorway, a handwritten sign made it extremely clear that my planned meeting with Emmett would have to wait: "Akasha temporarily closed until lunchtime."

Although frustrated by such a notice, a quick return from whence I had come would allow me to join George #111 in the café for our usual morning repast, as I had just left him in our chamber. With such an idea foremost in mind (and noting how hungry I had suddenly become), I turned and ran back down the corridor in the direction from which I had only just arrived. Unfortunately, when I turned into the first adjoining hallway, I ran right into Emma #119, nearly knocking her to the ground. The disaster was averted only because her fall was prevented by the tallest, ebony-colored man I had ever seen walking next to her. He grabbed her before she could stumble.

"Do you plan to make a habit of this? There is no running in the hallways!" she was not pleased. Once she had recovered, Emma leered over the rims of her black spectacles and seemed to be considering a number of possible ramifications.

"Emma, let's just go to the library," the tall man interjected. He reached his arm down to shake my hand and introduced himself, "I am Hakim #60."

I managed to say, "I am Ben #239," as I stared up at him, and then added quickly, "The library is closed until lunch."

Emma sounded even more irritated, "Young man, we are in the Core . . . the library is never closed for us."

"Let's go," Hakim said calmly. "Show me what you found."

She looked at me for a moment longer until speaking forcefully, "This is your second warning; I can assure you there will not be a third."

Emma took occasion to shake her head one final time, as the two passed and walked down the hallway in the direction of the library.

When I returned to my chamber, George was not there but I soon found him sitting at a table in the League café. Once I had acquired my usual fare of coffee, muffin, and honey, I sat across from him:

"You are never going to believe who I just ran into."

"Athena?"

"No, try again."

"The Governor-General?"

I chose to speak slowly: "Listen to what I am asking. Who do you think I just *ran* into?"

"Ah, got it. Was it Emma #119?" he appeared amused. "You just can't stay away from her, can you?"

"She was on her way to the library. She was with Hakim #60 – remember, Grimwald told us that he was the tallest individual in the Core? She was going to show him something."

"What?"

"I presume it has something to do with the records regarding England."

My roomie looked around briefly to assure that we were still alone before asking, "Have you found out anything more about Ruth?"

"Oh yes," I suddenly remembered, "Athena told me there was proof of some kind that Ruth was changing the ATL but she remains uncertain whether everyone believes it.

"What kind of proof?"

"I don't know. She said that the Horologium left a signature whenever we influenced a timeline."

He chuckled, "We can be followed, huh?"

"I asked Athena if the signature could be forged somehow but she didn't know."

George looked up from his plate, "What do you mean?"

"I don't know, somehow making the Horologium look like it was being used by someone else or coming from somewhere else?"

"You mean like VPN spoofing?" he asked seriously.

I looked at him in complete confusion, "I have absolutely no idea what you just said."

"I learned about it while doing research for the Gates' mission. On a computer, there are ways to disguise where you are coming from. You can do the same thing on a phone."

"Both were long after my time," I assured him.

"There is no time," my roomie reminded me. "Don't forget the line that becomes the dot."

As soon as George had spoken, the League emergency buzzer began sounding so loudly throughout the facility that I nearly jumped from my seat. The ringing prompted everyone within the café to immediately stop what they were doing. Most of those present hurriedly rushed from the room.

I quickly turned toward my roomie and said loud enough for him to hear, "Don't you think we should go to class?"

"Surely, there is another Wayfarer who can handle this? I haven't eaten yet."

"We better go just in case."

George reluctantly nodded. We left our dishes and breakfast in place and hastened toward the classroom (walking swiftly but not running). When we finally entered the room, Agnes appeared impatient. Whether it was due to the incessant noise or the fact that it took a while before my remaining classmates arrived, I was uncertain. When the noise finally came to an end, Agnes waved several pieces of paper in one hand before us. In her other hand, she gripped the stylus.

"I need a diplomat," Agnes bobbed about excitedly. We have to move quickly!" our instructress pointed the stylus directly at me. "This one is for you, Ben #239. Listen carefully, as you won't have an opportunity to visit the Akasha."

Agnes turned around and quickly wrote three words, underlining them before us: "Cuban Missile Crisis." When complete, she turned back in my direction, shook the pages with renewed vigor, and stated with certainty, "This is an emergency assignment from the ATL Mission Office. A problem has been created along multiple timelines."

Our instructress appeared even more distraught than during our last "emergency" situation. She glanced at the pieces of paper again, quickly mouthing the words as she reread the information before her. Finally, she gave voice to the briefing:

"The U.S.S.R. is sending nuclear ballistic missiles to Cuba. President John F. Kennedy is being advised to take direct military action. Such an approach will mean disaster!" Agnes slammed the pieces of paper on her desktop for emphasis. "You need to encourage a much calmer approach to this crisis. We need a diplomatic solution now!"

I nodded, stood from my seat, and went to her side. I took hold of my Horologium, turned the hands of the watch, stated the name that I had just heard, "John F. Kennedy," gave thought to the crisis, pressed the button, and became conscious of my fall.

I should note herein that if it were not for the necessity of always contemplating one's mission assignment during the journey, a time traveler might find some semblance of pleasure from the exhilaration of such a descent. I have found, unfortunately, that this thought is generally in the forefront of one's mind only after the mission has ended. When I next have occasion to become more cognizant of such an experience, I plan to avail myself of the opportunity.

Upon arriving at my destination, inhabiting the mind and body of the president, I became immediately aware that in spite of his youthful appearance the man's back was in severe pain. It was a constant pain, but rather than giving thought to his discomfort, the president focused instead upon the half a dozen men who surrounded him, all of whom had provided similar advice. From within the mind of Kennedy, I was soon able to discern the names of each, the positions they held, and their respective counsel:

General LeMay, the Air Force Chief of Staff, was adamant that military action was required. Joint Chiefs of Staff General Taylor was in favor of bombing known missile sites in Cuba as the first of several planned military responses. "Bobby," the president's brother, was certain that the ballistic missiles being sent via submarine by Khrushchev needed to be destroyed even before reaching Cuba's shoreline. Army Chief of Staff General Wheeler had suggested that an assault on Cuba, the occupation of the island, and the removal of Castro would all be necessary. Both Chief of Naval Operations Admiral George Anderson and Marine Commandant David Shoup agreed with each of the others; there was no choice but to meet the situation with an armed assault.

I became cognizant of these thoughts and the men who held them while managing to push aside the discomfort I felt within Kennedy's back. I gathered my own composure as a means of exploring the president's mind for some semblance of understanding of the entire situation in which I now found myself. It became immediately clear that Kennedy was the most cautious voice in the room, opting for an approach that first resolved why the Russians were sending missiles to Cuba in the first place. It was only after all this had come into my mind that I heard a woman's voice suddenly speak my name:

"Hello, Ben."

I gasped, turning my vaporous self in the direction of the words that had just been spoken. I saw the ghostly form of Ruth #7 standing before me.

"Ruth?" was all that came forth.

"We don't have much time," she said quickly, "and there is little I can say without affecting the timeline or providing information that will be recorded by the Akasha."

"How are you here?"

"She pointed to Bobby and the others. "I used a little influence, as I knew such a problem would bring forth a diplomat. I need to talk to you."

"What would you have me do?"

She appeared determined. "There is a solution for the president, and I believe there is one for myself. When I am gone, have the president seek the counsel of UN Ambassador Adlai Stevenson. Find a way to give time for diplomacy. Kennedy needs to discover a means of bargaining with Khrushchev – a win for both sides."

I nodded with understanding, "I am familiar with such an approach," and then inquired, "What can I do to help you?"

"Go to Milton #71; he can be trusted. Advise him that when the time is right, I will assist Mary."

"I do not understand," I said quickly.

Ruth replied, "Milton will understand. Tell him that I will assist Mary."

In the next instant, she was gone, disappearing completely from the room.

Let me simply make note of the fact that the Cuban crisis was resolved. Stevenson advised diplomacy. Kennedy authorized a blockade of the island. The blockade created time for both dialogue and resolution. In the end, the U.S.A. agreed not to invade Cuba. What would not be known for decades was that Kennedy had also agreed to remove his country's missiles from Turkey. The approach provided a win-win for both sides.

Once all manner of chaos and war had been averted, and I had occasion to tell Agnes #23 and the class an abbreviated account of my timeline journey (leaving out every mention of Ruth in the tale), I journeyed toward the ATL Mission Office. In addition to Ruth's assurance that Milton's allegiance would be favorably deposed in her direction, I remembered that Athena had shared her own appreciation of the man. As I entered the office door, I held in mind the hope that both were correct.

Athena looked up from her desk with some measure of surprise as I entered, "Are you here to see me?"

As I am prone to consider myself a diplomat in all matters of human interaction, I was moved to answer thusly: "Yes, I do want to see you but I also need to see Milton #71. Can I see you for dinner, and can I see him now?"

She smiled, rising from her chair, answering both questions with the statement: "Yes to dinner, and I think you can see him now." She turned toward Milton's door,

"Ben #239 would like to see you, if possible?"

"Absolutely!" came the English voice from the inner office.

I walked to his office doorway, just as he rose to greet me. He extended his hand across the desk and invited me to sit down.

"How can I help you?"

I chose to come quickly to the matter, "I need to speak with you about Ruth #7."

For a moment, he gave neither a response nor showed any sign of surprise. He simply sat quietly, looking intently upon me. What assumptions he was trying to deduce, I was unable to discern. What I do know is that he spoke only after an exceedingly long period of silence.

"Perhaps you should close the door?"

I arose to do as he requested, and then retook my seat.

"What do you know about Ruth?" came his inquiry.

"I believe she is in trouble," were the first words that came to me. "I think someone is changing the ATL and attempting to make her look responsible." I pulled out my Horologium and showed him the etching within ("Help!R7"). To be sure, it did not seem prudent to relate the fact that I myself had told her to make such an inscription. I said only, "She asked for my help. She is in trouble."

There was silence again as he continued to watch me. By the time he finally chose to speak, I had become most uncomfortable. He finally replied, "Ben, I have come to the very same conclusion."

I leaned forward in my chair, "Have you told anyone else?"

"I have not. The situation requires discretion and caution."

I volunteered, "We could use my watch as proof."

Milton quickly interjected, "We cannot. What if we inadvertently told the very ones responsible? We have no way of knowing how many may be involved."

"Surely there is something you can do?"

Milton #71 rubbed his hands together as he spoke, "This is problematic from every angle of consideration. I have given the matter a great deal of thought and still do not know what I can do. Something must be done but the solution continues to escape me."

"Once you are in the meeting of the Core, you could tell everyone that someone is doing this to Ruth."

Milton leaned forward, folding his hands before him. "Imagine that I tell the entire Core of my suspicions. While other members of the Core are investigating such a possibility, whoever is responsible could simply go back and make certain that I am no more. And if I did not exist, then I would never have told my suspicions to the Core in the first place. There would be a reset."

I chose to inquire, "Is this not the very method used by the Core to eradicate someone from the League?"

Milton was quick to respond, "Absolutely not! That approach is far too dangerous to the stability of the Akasha, the League, and the school."

I theorized a solution, "Can you inform the Core and have several Wayfarers go back to make certain that nothing interferes with the time of your recruitment?"

"Yes, that would work for the one moment of my recruitment," Milton agreed, "but there are many ways to eliminate a potential adversary from the timeline."

"How?"

"Have you heard of the 'Grandfather paradox?'" he inquired.

"I have not."

"Imagine you go back and accidentally kill your grandfather in his youth, thereby preventing your own birth in the future. All an individual would have to do is to go back and kill your grandfather, your father, or your mother at any point before you were born. Once that occurs, any memory of your presence here at the League would be completely eliminated."

"But what about Ruth?" I asked finally. "The Core is meeting to decide what to do with her."

"Yes," Milton agreed, "and I have wondered whether there may be a way to use that as an advantage."

"What do you mean?"

"Obviously, whoever is responsible would prefer that the Core remove Ruth from the League, rather than having to do it themselves?"

"Why?"

"Removing Ruth has the potential to create any number of paradoxes – with the school, with the curriculum, with all those who have graduated. If the one responsible for these ATL changes has to eliminate Ruth themself, it is unimaginable what might occur. However, if the Core is forced to do it, returning her to one hour after her recruitment, then the fact that she has been here will remain a part of the record, the curriculum remains intact, and no changes occur to all those who have passed through the school."

"I spoke with Ruth on my last mission," I finally confessed.

Milton appeared surprised but inquired nonetheless, "What did she say?"

"She said that you could be trusted. She told me to tell you that when the time is right, she will assist Mary."

Milton stopped speaking and contemplated the words I had just spoken. While in the midst of such introspection, there was a knock at the door. Athena opened it slightly and peeked within:

"You told me to alert you to any ATL changes on the

Elizabethan timeline as soon as possible."

"Yes?" Milton sat up quickly and motioned for her to continue.

Athena responded, "I have been watching the record and I just found a new change. It appears that the queen gave Walter Raleigh a charter, granting him authority, and I am quoting: 'to discover, explore, and establish a colony on the east coast of the New World.' The ATL now indicates that within three years of the charter, an expedition settles upon Roanoke Island, a landmass off the coast."

Milton turned in my direction, appearing more troubled than I had previously witnessed, "The expansion continues."

For a time, your perception of self will remain unchanged. You will see yourself as you were. Your thoughts will remain your own. You will even possess memories of your own illusory journey along the timeline of your life's experience. All these things will attest to the presumption that you remain now the very individual of whom you have always been aware. And yet, this perception is but a faint reflection of a far greater reality.

Beyond the confines of what you once believed about yourself, beyond every limitation once placed upon you by self or another, and beyond every regret or desire you once held in mind resides an awareness of a much greater Truth just waiting to be awakened. That is the Self that becomes part of the WHOLE, and wholeness remains our goal for every sentient being.

Excerpt, "Perceiving the Self," *A Time Traveler's Code of Conduct* **by Ruth #7**

TEN: *Journal Entry – April 26 ATL*

I have been derelict in my vow to make note of activities here at the school for the past few days but such neglect was not intended. I found myself overtaken by classwork and other matters of concern; however, the respite did provide the opportunity to review the curriculum with George prior to our "midterm" (as Agnes #23 is extremely fond of calling her lengthy examination), and I was able to follow through on my promised dinner with Athena.

Athena now occupies my wandering thoughts much more frequently than I would have imagined. Although I have long found myself afflicted with a weakness for the other sex, my connection with her feels very different than anything I have previously experienced. I must admit that I find this fact both enchanting and troubling. In truth, I am delighted by the possibility of seeing her whether through happenstance or design but I find myself troubled because I think of little else.

The evening meal we shared between us provided the most charming opportunity to relate our pasts to one another and our life experiences prior to our respective recruitments. I gave voice to my own background in invention and printing and diplomacy; she surprised me with details of her scholarly training and the fact that she had once worked in a learned facility at Alexandria. Two surprises also occurred during our meal, which I detail, as follows:

The first became evident the moment we arrived at the café. I noticed that Emma #119 and Hakim #60 were also present, eating with one another. Although it was apparent that Emma saw me enter the café, she refused to acknowledge my presence at any time during the meal, choosing instead to consistently look in another direction. For much of the evening, I strained repeatedly to ascertain what the two might be discussing but heard nothing. It was only when they were leaving (with Emma turning away even as they passed our table) that I heard Hakim utter the very words I had learned in Milton's office but a few days previous: "Roanoke Island."

The second surprise came as we were finishing our repast when Athena inquired as to whether I was amenable to the idea of having a date experience in a locale "far from the League facility."

"How do we do that?" I found myself pondering the very idea as soon as the question was asked.

She twirled her hair around a fingertip, "It is very

simple. We choose a place and time and look for a couple sharing a meal between them. They become our targets."

"Is such an experience not crowded with the thoughts of another?"

"Sure, but you can still have fun and you can still speak your own thoughts. You experience whatever the couple experiences plus your own sensations . . ." She added quickly, "You can taste the food."

The idea certainly intrigued me, and I soon inquired, "I would imagine that such a connection with said target need not be limited to the meal?"

"You are correct; it need not be limited," she smiled.

I held in mind the very possibilities provided by such a time travel endeavor long after the night was over.

At last, I found time and occasion to return to the library and speak with Emmett. Upon my arrival, I saw him in conversation with two individuals I had never laid eyes upon before – a refined-looking gentleman and a stately woman with an abundance of hair. Emmett continued to speak with the couple as he waved an acknowledgment in my direction. Since he was engaged in conversation, I followed the pathway of one of the book corridors as a part of my wait. I looked for nothing in particular, simply gazing in wonderment at such an incredible selection of volumes. I found myself wandering through the passageway for quite some time and had almost decided to begin researching some topic in regard to Queen Elizabeth herself when Emmett made his appearance.

"I apologize for the delay," the old man said upon his arrival. "I was speaking to two members of the Core."

"Who were they?"

"The gentleman is Lucius #19. The woman is Mia #161. They are here for the Core meeting."

I acknowledged his words while making certain that we were alone, "I understand. Did you find out any more about Grimwald or Emma?"

The old man appeared weary as he spoke, "Emma has been here twice with Hakim #60. Whatever she is doing, she is involving him as well. I believe Grimwald may be sharing whatever he thinks he knows with Sara #11."

"Why do you say that?"

"She came to see me," he said somberly, "inquiring about the approved timeline for Walter Raleigh, an English statesman and explorer. I discovered it to be the very topic Grimwald himself had discussed with her."

"Does it have something to do with Roanoke Island?"

Emmett appeared completely perplexed, "How do you know of such a place?"

I said only, "I heard Hakim mention it to Emma in the café."

The old man paused for a moment before adding, "This has become far more complex than I might have imagined. It may be our adversary did not envision that these plans would come to anyone's attention. When something is in accord with the ATL, it generally proceeds without notice."

"What can we do?"

"I am uncertain as to what should be done. I am afraid that things appear quite problematic for Ruth #7. Both Lucius and Mia are convinced that she has been manipulating the timeline."

"It does not make any sense. Ruth is central to the school and the League. She would not do such a thing! I know it. I truly know it," I was near to describing my own meeting with Milton when Emmett interrupted:

"I have known Ruth for a very long time," he sighed. "It was I who recruited her . . . a very, very long time ago. She would never be capable of such betrayal."

"Why would anybody seek power from a queen whose term will come to an end. Some day she is going to die. Such control would be limited at best."

"You are mistaken," Emmett responded quickly. "A Wayfarer could simply transfer oversight to whoever comes next. After Elizabeth, James I ascends the throne."

A thought came to mind, which I spoke aloud, "Since it is history that is being changed, perhaps we should talk to Milton #71 . . .?"

Emmett was quick to interrupt, "You cannot talk to anyone on the Core! We do not yet know who is involved."

I sighed, wondering for a moment whether my meeting with Milton had been a mistake after all, "What do you want me to do?"

The old man pondered the question before concluding, "I need to speak with every member of the Core." He looked straight into my eyes, "I will have a discussion with each of them, stating that I wish to assist in this issue of their meeting. I may be able to discover who truly needs to become the focus of our concern."

I only nodded, contemplating the seriousness of what lay before us.

Agnes #23 eagerly gripped her stylus and proceeded to write and underline the words "Village of Kersey" on the whiteboard before us. She appeared extremely pleased as she informed the class, "Today I am happy to share with you the case history of the Medieval time slip!" She waved the stylus before us as she emphasized the fact, "This happened in the space-time illusion of 1957 when three teenage British Naval Cadets somehow journeyed more than five hundred years into a perception of the past!"

"Can you imagine, five hundred years?" She slapped the top of her desk, causing several of my classmates to jump in alarm. "Now you should know that in the village of Kersey, the most noticeable building has long been the tower of Saint Mary's Church. It rises far above the trees and can be seen in the village from every direction." Agnes lifted her hand far into the air in an effort to demonstrate the height of such a structure. When the height had been thoroughly established, she held up three fingers to inform us, "These three cadets had arrived at Kersey to take part in a map reading exercise as part of their training. Their names were Ray Baker, Michael Crowley, and William Laing." Our instructress made note of such upon the board and continued:

"Upon their arrival in the village, the young men became immediately aware that something was very strange. They heard no sounds. There was no wind. There was no sign of twentieth-century life – no automobiles or people or phone lines or overhead wires. The road was completely deserted. The houses were all made of rough and ragged timber and appeared to be hand-built. They looked old, even ancient. One of the young men told the others, 'This place is medieval!'"

For the benefit of the class, Agnes paced back and forth in front of the whiteboard as a means of emphasizing what came next, "As they walked up the main street, they were surprised to find no pub or meeting house off in the distance, nor could they see the tower of the central church that had been described to them." She interrupted herself to remind us, "Remember, they had been told by their commanding officer that the tower of Saint Mary's could be seen from all corners of the village."

The pacing and our teacher's description continued: "The three cadets walked to the first building and looked into dirty, mold-covered windows. Hanging from a beam on the ceiling were several ox carcasses that appeared old and green and withered with age. The cadets spoke between themselves that it appeared to be a meat market or butcher shop of some kind but the conditions were obviously primitive."

"They peered into the dirty windows of the next dwelling, which looked as if it were a house." The stylus was nearly thrown from her hand as she shook it to underscore the fact that, "No one was there either! The walls had been unevenly painted with whitewash but they could see no table or chairs or possessions of any kind. There was no modern convenience or any sign that the building had electricity. It was ancient. They continued down the main street. As they looked around at the buildings, everything was dated. From all they could see, the village of Kersey seemed deserted. They were frightened by the strangeness of such a place, and the three became scared. One suggested to the others that they needed to run. Without hesitation, the cadets hurried away from the place."

Agnes quickened her steps as if to sprint before us, "They ran back down the street and arrived at the very edge of town. All at once, they began to hear the ringing of a church bell. They turned around (our instructress demonstrated such a turn) and in the distance saw the church tower that had not been there just a moment before. They felt the breeze in the air and could hear the singing of birds. They saw phone lines overhead, smoke rising from a few of the chimneys, and several cars were parked along the roadway before them."

She stopped moving about, looking upon each of us one by one, "Obviously, they were scared. Something had happened to them but they did not know what. They hurried from Kersey as fast as they could. When they returned to their commanding officer, they told him all that they had witnessed, each describing the very same scene. In the end, their commander simply laughed, assuring the cadets that the village of Kersey was simply very old."

"Do you know what happened next?" Agnes responded to her own query, "Nearly forty years would pass. The story was told to anyone who would listen. Finally, a British writer and researcher named Andrew MacKenzie heard the tale and interviewed each of the cadets, who were now in their fifties. MacKenzie visited the village of Kersey for himself and would come to discover that the nearest building at the edge of town – the one they had described as a butcher shop – was actually a house. But do you know what he discovered during his research? Prior to 1790, it had been a butcher shop!" Agnes slapped the top of her desk with vigor. "And it had also been built in the 1300s."

"What is also interesting," she assured us, "is that MacKenzie determined the village had been decimated by the Black Death, the bubonic plague. The plague had killed most of the villagers, leaving much of it deserted for years. The plague was the very reason the town had appeared abandoned," Agnes bobbed about with excitement, "and they hadn't seen the church tower because it hadn't been built yet! Apparently, the lack of villagers had halted construction on the church tower for decades. It was MacKenzie who finally theorized that their visit had taken them to 1420 – before the church tower had been completed!"

Our instructor stopped moving about and pointed her stylus at each of us in turn. "Do you know that MacKenzie even wrote a book that included this story? It was called 'Adventures in Time' and still, most individuals have never even heard about it. The book went out of print shortly after it was published."

She shook her head in disgust, "How so many people can continue to be ignorant about this topic is absolutely astonishing to me!"

Once the day's scheduled events had finally come to conclusion, and I had taken the opportunity to speak with both George and Athena in regard to my plans, I took the Horologium in hand for an excursion. Recent events had prompted the need for action, involving a background mission of my own design. The destination was to be Roanoke Island, and my intended target was the colonial governor, one John White (a name that Athena had obligingly provided from her own examination of the timeline). I found myself uncertain as to whether the proposed mission came as a result of the desire to possess additional facts regarding the matter or was simply an impulsive attempt to become helpful in a situation in which I felt of very little use. What had become entirely clear, however, was the fact that I needed to do something.

After following the required procedure and allowing myself some small measure of enjoyment from the descending fall, I arrived within the consciousness of John White, my intended target. Although I had given little thought to the destination of Roanoke Island before setting the hands of the watch, my first impression was less than favorably inclined. The location was truly primitive.

The colony had taken refuge within a hastily-constructed fort, nigh unto the shape of an enormous square. The rudimentary walls were less than the height of a man with pointed bastions (like arrowheads) on three of the four sides, seemingly allowing whoever might be standing guard to have a greater view of oversight for defense. The fourth side of the fort (where another bastion might have been erected) opened unto the beachfront, perhaps as a means of enabling small boats to be pulled within the confines and the protection of the surrounding walls. There were several structures that appeared to be makeshift dwellings, mostly comprised of timber, rock, and soil. Numerous tents had also been positioned within the fort's walls, and from the placement of blankets scattered upon the ground, it was apparent that at least some had taken to sleeping out of doors.

I made note of perhaps twenty women and children but knew from John White's thoughts that 117 others had undertaken the journey with him. I understood that the men and older boys were elsewhere employed, in search of food (fish and game) and their ongoing attempts to learn what they could from peaceful relations with the Indians. As I watched my ghostly form continuously envelop the body of my target, I allowed whatever thoughts White held in mind to become my own, and his thoughts were numerous.

He had been hired by Walter Raleigh himself to make the journey and to serve as governor upon arriving in the New World. The island had not been his intended locale for the colony and he had been reluctant to remain, believing that northward toward the Chesapeake would be more hospitable in terms of the environment and natives. However, the ship's captain, one Simon Fernandes, had argued vehemently against continuing the journey and White had reluctantly allowed all to remain. The ship and its travelers and cargo had been upon the island for more than a month, and in the interim, they had befriended members of both the Roanoke and Croatan Indian tribes.

In addition to the inhospitable wilderness and the questions arising from countless unknowns, multiple problems came to the governor's mind. The colonists' supplies were lower than required to get through a long winter. Although they had planted crops, thus far rain was sparse while intense heat remained plentiful. There was a shortage of women, as the men outnumbered them nearly seven to one – not an ideal situation for either the creation of a colony or the appeasement of males. I knew from my exploration of the thoughts White held in mind that he was no longer favored among the colonists as any semblance of leader. If the governor had not already known his standing with the colonists, it had become clear when the majority presented a petition signed by most that he be among those sent back to England in pursuit of additional supplies and whatever women might be willing to make the four-month journey.

Rather than laboring in matters of oversight and the direction of other men, it was apparent that John

White most preferred to be engaged in the creation of illustrations, for he was truly an artist. It was clear that drawing was his passion, second only to his love of family. Although his wife was long dead, his daughter, Eleanor Dare, and her husband, Ananias, numbered themselves among the colonists, and 26 days after their arrival, on August 18, 1587, the couple had given birth to a child, Virginia Dare (named for the Virgin Queen), who was already heralded as the first English child born in the New World. John White was delighted to be a grandfather.

It was only after all of these thoughts had entered my mind that I heard a woman scream:

"Ben #239! What are you doing here?"

I jumped and turned, observing the black-rimmed spectacles before I even saw the vaporous forms of Emma and Hakim standing before me.

"You are in serious trouble now!" was all she said to me.

"What were you doing on Roanoke Island?" Emma #119's words were spoken angrily as she pointed at me from across the table. She repeated herself, "What were you doing?"

We were in Meeting Room 2, near the administrative offices. Emma and Hakim #60 sat on one side of the table. (Even while sitting, Hakim towered nearly a head above us.) The Governor-General, Sara #11, and I sat on the other. Looking upon the faces that surrounded me, it was clear that Emma was mad, while Hakim and Sara appeared very much confused by the situation.

"Yes, Ben, what were you doing?" Sara inquired for herself.

I replied, "I wanted to do a background assignment to see what was happening on the island."

Emma was quick to ask, "And where did you hear of Roanoke Island in the first place?"

I sat quietly until the Governor-General repeated the question, "Where did you hear of Roanoke Island, Ben?"

"From the two of them," I pointed across the table at Hakim and Emma. I thought it wisest not to mention the fact that Athena had first mentioned the place in Milton's office.

"What?" Emma #119 replied angrily. "We have never spoken with you about this!"

"I heard you talking about it in the League café."

Sara looked toward the two. Emma appeared perplexed but Hakim nodded while acknowledging, "That is very likely."

I looked directly at Emma, "What were you doing on Roanoke Island?" I asked in return.

Sara repeated, "Yes, Emma what were you and Hakim doing there?"

Emma was not pleased with the question, "A background mission! We were trying to see who else was involved with Ruth's violation of protocols." Emma peered over her spectacles and looked at me directly, "I thought there might also be a meeting place in the past. That's when we caught him."

The Governor-General asked, "What did you think you would find, Ben?"

"I thought it might have something to do with helping Ruth," I replied.

"He is lying!" Emma was still noticeably upset. "He is working with Ruth. I know it!"

Hakim looked at me directly, "What do you think Ruth needs help with?"

My own statement had prompted his question. I needed to refrain from the implication of anyone else, as the unknowns continued to remain too numerous. I took the Horologium from my pocket, opened the facing of the watch, and pointed out the etching ("Help!R7") as I passed it to Sara.

The Governor-General held my mechanism within her hands for only a moment before speaking, "This is most curious."

Emma was impatient, "Let me see."

Sara passed the pocket watch to Emma, who passed it in turn to Hakim #60.

It was Hakim who finally spoke, "I may need to reconsider my thoughts on Ruth's involvement."

"How do we know this isn't part of their plan?" Emma was still upset. She pointed back in my direction, "I am certain he is involved. I'm certain of it."

Sara appeared more understanding, "Obviously, he is involved. It would appear that Ruth wrote a request for help in his Horologium." She quickly turned in my direction, "She did put this in your watch, right Ben?"

"Yes, in my old chamber, when she gave it to me."

She added, "Is that why you have been asking about her?"

"Yes, I didn't say more last time because I was uncertain who might be involved."

Hakim's thoughts were spoken aloud, "It would seem we have all been entertaining the very same dilemma: Who is responsible?"

Emma was not convinced, "Ruth's own Horologium has revealed her responsibility! She was tracked! She is definitely involved."

"What about VPN spoofing?" I asked quickly, only

partially cognizant of what I had even said.

The Governor-General chose to respond, "I don't think you can fool the Akasha, Ben. However, I don't believe Ruth would have done this either. That is the problem. All evidence points to Ruth's involvement but a few of us believe . . ." (Sara looked right at Emma as she spoke) "Ruth could not possibly be involved." After a moment, she added, "I would like to speak with Ben #239 alone."

Emma #119 was angered by the request, upset that she was not to be a part of whatever came next. Hakim #60 calmly nodded with understanding. When they had left the room, Sara leaned closer and looked into my eyes:

"Ben, I think you know more than you are telling me. You are going to have to trust someone. When you need help, you come to me. Okay?"

I had been involved with diplomacy long enough to ascertain that her words were spoken with sincerity. For that reason, I responded in agreement, "Yes, Miss Sara. I will come to see you when I need help."

The days that followed became filled with all manner of complication and activity on my part. Aside from the usual schedule of class time and follow-up assignments, I found occasion for two encounters with Athena, both of which resulted in the most delightful personal time between us. I also undertook a meeting with Emmett, followed by another with Milton, keeping both informed of my recent interaction with the Governor-General,

Emma, and Hakim. As I evidently seemed much more anxious than usual, my roomie expressed his concern regarding my harried behavior, prompting me to promise to keep him informed on every development. It was a promise I kept fully as it concerned my encounters with Emmett, members of the Core, and my experience on Roanoke Island but only partially as it involved Athena. George seemed particularly interested in the colonists and could not refrain from wondering aloud about their fate.

I had related similar accounts to Emmett, who listened thoughtfully to the John White excursion and my interaction with Sara #11 and the others, which followed. He was quick to remind me that it remained unclear as to who could be trusted and repeated his own plan to continue his interactions with all members of the Core. He was somber as he related the fact that everyone with whom he had discussed the issue could not see beyond Ruth's guilt, as neither the Horologium nor the Akasha was capable of deceit.

Milton had listened to my story as well, and upon hearing my conviction that the Governor-General was in no way involved in the situation, resolved that the time had come for a meeting between the three of us. That decision gave rise to Sara, Milton, and I sitting together in the ATL Mission Office, with Milton choosing to speak first:

"Sara, thank you for coming to see us. Ben has informed me of your recent meeting with him, and both of us believe we need your help."

For a few moments, the Governor-General looked between us. I was sitting next to her, while Milton sat on the other side of his desk. After repeatedly glancing between us, she finally spoke, "I knew there was more going on than you were telling me, Ben."

"We may be among the few who remain convinced of Ruth's innocence," Milton #71 asserted, "so I would recommend we devise a plan before the meeting of the Core."

Sara interjected, "The Core meets in two days, Milton. What do you propose?"

"I have an idea as to how we might capture whoever is responsible." Milton sounded convinced, "We can seize the culprit in the act."

"What do you mean?" I asked, even before Sara could speak.

"I know where Ruth is going to be, and I know what she is planning to do," came his reply.

The Governor-General was stunned, "What are you talking about?"

"She sent me a message, through Ben."

Sara looked toward me, appearing less than pleased that I knew far more than she had previously imagined. Nonetheless, she inquired, "What is she planning to do?"

Milton nodded, "She is going to change the ATL and create an emergency in the process."

"What?" Sara appeared concerned. "She is going to do the very thing for which she is being charged. To what end?"

"So that we might reveal who is truly responsible." He paused, looking at me from across the desk, "We are also going to need Athena's help." He seemed pleased with himself before speaking the one concern he still held in mind: "If only we could get a message to Ruth #7. This might work best during the very meeting of the Core."

An idea quickly came into my mind, "I can get a message to Ruth. Leave that to me."

After every aspect of the plan had been discussed between us, I took hold of my Horologium and chose to revisit my own mission assignment within the president's office, the occasion of my last meeting with Ruth. I turned the hands of the watch in a counterclockwise direction, repeated "John F. Kennedy" several times over, and gave thought to the crisis as it had existed prior to my own rectification. On this occasion, however, curiosity had gotten hold of me. I now had an opportunity to encounter a version of my previous self. With that in mind, I chose to press "TEMPUS" only once, took a breath, and began to fall. Although my mind remained focused mostly upon the matters at hand, I did allow myself to become conscious of the sensation of wind whipping past my body as I plummeted toward the ground.

Upon my arrival, I became aware of my previous self as well as the intensity of pain within Kennedy's own back. It was immediately obvious that I had caught my previous self by complete surprise, as the former me asked aloud: "Is that you? Ben?"

"It is I," I quickly admitted.

As the president was not on the verge of personal demise, it took some semblance of effort on my part to separate myself from the president (as well as my former self) but I finally managed to do so, turned back to look upon my other ghostly form and stated, "Curiosity got the best of me."

"Truly, I understand," the former me replied. "I have been wondering about such an experience. Was the mission not a success?"

"It was indeed a success. I am here for another reason." I motioned toward my former self as its vaporous form moved in waves of transparent energy around the body of the president, "Go ahead with your assessment. I will wait."

I watched my other self as he gave thought to the names of the very advisors I had encountered only a week earlier and the counsel they had provided: General LeMay, General Taylor, "Bobby," General Wheeler, Admiral Anderson, and Marine Commandant Shoup, all recommending immediate military action. Without exception, each had been completely wrong. I gave the previous me an opportunity to evaluate the entire mission and come to this very same conclusion. As that occurred, I chose to look about the room as I called to mind Ruth's words from the text: *"Once interaction with a timeline has occurred, space-time is altered ever so slightly."*

The room appeared somewhat different than during my previous visit. The blue carpet was imprinted with the image of an enormous eagle and I couldn't help but wonder, "Hadn't the carpet been green before?" I made note of the individuals around me and was very much certain that each appeared much more disheveled than during our last encounter: "Are they even wearing the same clothes?" I made note of a globe upon the president's desk (a spherical image of the earth) and remained confident that no such globe had been present earlier.

I was near unto finishing my assessment of the changes I could see, making note to myself to take more care in the perception of these things on mission assignments, just as my former self appeared to complete his own appraisal of the situation. All at once, I heard a woman's voice speak the name:

"Hello, Ben #239," followed by "Ben?" as she gazed upon the second image of myself.

"Ruth?" came forth from my previous self.

I quickly interjected, "Let me speak quickly, then the two of you may fix the problems before you."

Ruth turned in my direction as I continued, "Ruth, you need to tell my previous self what you came to say, and I need to tell you what transpires within the Core."

Ruth nodded, and I quickly discussed the reason for my return. When I had finished providing her with the appropriate timetable, I turned to myself and stated, "It is quite good to see you."

The previous version of myself proceeded to give the very same acknowledgment in return, prompting Ruth to state, "We don't have much time, and there is little I can say without affecting the timeline or providing information that will be recorded by the Akasha."

I pressed "TEMPUS" three times over, making the journey home.

The Collective Illusion contains every manner of diversion and possibility. The yearning of such fascinations and desires may long be a part of personal awareness, should one be capable of turning loose of such thoughts at all. For some, the allure will reside ever within one's consciousness but remain unexpressed. For others, the ongoing desire eventually overshadows even the awareness that these things are simply a portion of the illusion itself, and they will falter.

You are a part of the Time Traveler's League. You are instrumental in what we must accomplish. The appeal of anything other than the greater good of the WHOLE is only an impediment to your own growth and our ultimate goal. Without you, and those like you, that which we hope to attain remains forever beyond our reach. You have been entrusted by the Core for a mission that began at the moment of your recruitment. Hold fast to the reason you were granted the opportunity before you. In so doing, you will ever choose what is right.

Excerpt, "Choosing Darkness or Choosing Light," *A Time Traveler's Code of Conduct* by Ruth #7

ELEVEN: *Journal Entry – April 29 ATL*

"This is so exciting! So very exciting!" Agnes paced back and forth before the class appearing nearly unable to control herself. "You know the Core is meeting right now! The WHOLE Core! It is just so exciting!"

As the purpose of the meeting had yet to be communicated to my classmates (and only George and I possessed any measure of familiarity with the issue), Manuela #64 inquired, "So why are they meeting?"

"Obviously, Core business!" Agnes was quick to reply. "Don't you understand that there is important Core business?" She shook her head in frustration and looked about her desk seemingly in an effort to remember what curriculum had been scheduled for the day's agenda. Before Agnes had even managed to take stylus in hand, however, the emergency alarm went off, prompting even our instructress to jump in surprise.

The buzzer rang loudly throughout the entire facility. There had been no doubt in the minds of anyone involved in the planning that such an interruption would bring the Core meeting to a complete halt. The incessant sound of ringing continued as Agnes looked repeatedly toward the classroom door waiting for news from the ATL Mission Office as to the nature of the emergency and what was to be done about it. When it appeared that the deafening alarm was without end and we could take the horrendous noise no longer, Athena finally arrived at the classroom doorway holding papers in hand. She passed the pages to Agnes #23 while speaking loud enough for the benefit of all present, "This emergency assignment has just arrived."

Athena turned to wink in my direction before turning to leave. Our teacher stood silent, mouthing the words on the pages before her as she read. While still absorbed in the review of what she had been handed, the alarm finally came to an end.

Agnes read and reread the papers clutched between her hands. When she finally spoke, her voice was filled with concern, "This is a big one! We have no choice but to move quickly!" She shook the papers before us, "It has been a long while since I have seen one like this!" As she bobbed about, she explained the emergency situation and what was to be done:

"Ben #239, problems are erupting on timelines

VI, XLII, and LXXV. Elizabeth I failed to sign a death warrant executing Mary Queen of Scots. Mary will soon have assistance escaping from Fotheringhay Castle, and there will be a plan to place her upon the British throne. We need a diplomat to set right the entire course of English history!"

I began to get up from my seat in order to walk to the front of the room but Agnes responded by holding her palm out in my direction, prompting my delay.

"Wait, there is more," she said nervously. She glanced back at the pages between her hands and continued with the recommended course of action: "Emanuel #41, a dozen timelines are showing major disruptions in Anglican Church history, and a push for the revival of Catholicism throughout the British empire. I need you to fix this immediately, or there will be problems on more timelines than I have time to count!"

Emanuel started to rise when Agnes held up her palm for a second time and exclaimed, "Wait, there's more." She glanced first toward the pages and then turned to our French classmate: "Bonne Souer Marie #304, this one is for you too! A majority of the English noble class plans to revolt if Mary assumes the throne. Along timelines XVII, LXVII, and LXXXI, the Protestant Armada is assembling as it waits for a possible attack from its Spanish counterpart. Elizabeth I is calling all ships home to assist the English. If there is war, countless individuals will die or be wounded . . . I need a healer!"

Agnes motioned for the three of us to come to the front of the room as she walked nervously about, "You have prepared for assignments like this. You know what you are doing! You do know what you are doing?" As I stood with Emanuel and Bonne Souer Marie, I heard my roomie turn to Manuela #64 and say, "I know some individuals who are going to need our help. Come with me."

☒ ☒ ☒

In spite of the fact that my own travels as Wayfarer have been relatively short in duration, already I have had occasion to inhabit the mind of several heads of state on these various mission assignments. I found each to be very different, one from another, whether it be an Egyptian Pharaoh, two British Kings, or an American President.

Certainly, my experience with Ramesses was unlike anything I had previously encountered, not only due to the novelty of my experience in such matters of time travel but owing to the circumstance that no other ruler thus far has been so focused upon self. When I encountered King George V, more than anything else his motivation had been one of duty toward England. For King Edward VIII, love and affection remained his greatest desires, perhaps as he had never received same in his youth. As I aided Kennedy in the Cuban crisis, he felt a calling to move his country toward a new generation of wellbeing, with hopes for the future which may have appeared all but improbable to some. The situation I found within Elizabeth I's own state of mind was very different than anything that had gone before.

As I desired to go back and arrive before Ruth #7 changed the timeline, I chose to appear within the consciousness of the Queen even before the death warrant was before her. Upon my arrival, it was readily apparent that Elizabeth felt surrounded on every side by deception and intrigue. Such duplicity had prompted her to exercise extreme caution at all times, especially in matters of state. She had become a brilliant statesman and was more educated and wise than many who had preceded her. She had an aptitude for discerning much that transpired within palace walls (and beyond) and had become a champion of moderation in all things. Whether it was a means of lessening the threat of those who might choose to oppose her at every turn or was simply a part of her own temperament, it was an approach that had given rise to her motto: "Video et taceo" ("I see and keep silent").

As England had gone through one ruler after another (Henry, Edward, Jane, Mary Tudor, and Philip), for years her survival before her own coronation had been more a matter of luck than design. Already, she had been the focus of three assassination attempts, and the pope had chosen to excommunicate her, calling into question the very legitimacy of her reign. While her own Protestant ministers repeatedly found occasion to remind her of the duty to marry (providing both a king and a male child as heir), Catholics continued to revile her. Adding to all of these challenges, and in spite of her many talents as ruler, her image of self was less than flattering.

I felt Elizabeth's fingers touch the disfigured skin of her pocked face. Her neck and cheeks were filled with the familiar scars I knew to be smallpox – scars she tried to cover each and every day with the thick, white makeup that those who attended her helped put in place. She felt loneliness and jealousy and a longing to be with another but at the same time went to great lengths to keep herself apart. Although men were essential in all matters of state, she rarely felt comfortable in their presence and repeatedly refrained from all but the fewest of relationships. Whether the matter was due most to the unwanted advances of Thomas Seymour in her youth (a married man twenty-five years her senior who had pursued her at fifteen), her own precarious position as Queen, or the fact that she had witnessed more than her share of marriages and betrayals, she vowed to remain a virgin. At the same time, she found herself completely drawn to a few: Robert Dudley, Walter Raleigh, Francis Drake, and others.

Elizabeth stood in her cabinet room within Whitehall Palace, waiting for the arrival of her secretary, William Davison. As she possessed no desire to sign the warrant authorizing the death of Mary, Queen of Scots, time and again she had delayed this very moment. Although Mary had been found guilty of conspiracy in the most recent assassination attempt, Elizabeth had her reasons for hesitation.

The two were cousins and had once considered themselves friends. Setting aside their connection, Elizabeth feared the execution of a Catholic Queen would lead to even bigger problems – problems with the pope, problems with Catholics throughout Europe, problems with Scotland. The list went on. She deeply abhorred the idea of regicide, for killing a monarch undoubtedly brought with it the rath of both history and divine will. Above all things, she desired a reign known for the growth of England and the flourishing of the arts – poetry, music, and drama – not the death of a rival.

After all these thoughts had passed through her mind, I pushed myself from her being and managed to stand apart from the queen herself. Although I had known little about her prior to my journey, I suddenly had immense respect for the woman before me. In all matters of governance, Elizabeth I was indeed a queen.

Within a matter of moments, William Davison entered the room. He held the death warrant within in his hand. Just as the vaporous self of Ruth #7 enveloped the queen's presence, Davison placed the warrant next to the quill and ink upon the table before them.

"Mary has been found guilty in this matter," Davison told Elizabeth. "I fear you no longer have any choice but to sign."

The queen stood for a moment before finally nodding in reluctance. I watched as Ruth's ghostly form closed her eyes and seemingly gave focus to another thought within Elizabeth's own mind. Even as the queen took quill in one hand and moved to take the warrant in the other, Ruth's eyes remained closed. As I was familiar with these matters of influencing a timeline target, it was clear what Ruth was doing. The result came just as Elizabeth was about to dip the quill in the inkstand before her. She suddenly placed the quill on the table and allowed the warrant to fall from her hand.

"No!" she said forcefully. "I will not be responsible for this."

Ruth opened her eyes and looked to me as she spoke, "I would imagine that the alarm has already been sounded."

"It has," I agreed.

"Let me speak to make certain this becomes a part of the records, as I know there are those watching the Akasha." She appeared to think about it for only a moment before stating aloud, "I, Ruth #7, plan to alter the timeline of all English history."

When her words had been spoken, we both stood quiet. It was I who finally inquired, "How long before someone comes?"

"Undoubtedly, it will happen momentarily," came her reply.

As we spoke, Davison tried to give every manner of reason to the queen. His arguments were numerous.

There was no other possible course of action. Such was in the best interest of Elizabeth's reign. Parliament itself had found Mary guilty. The Protestant nobles would take offense at such delay. Spain would use Mary as a pawn to place a Catholic upon the throne. While he went through the litany of his concerns and had even begun to repeat himself, Queen Elizabeth simply watched, waiting for him to finish.

All at once, the ghostly presence of five others came before us. There was Emma, and Hakim, and Grimwald, and Sara, and Milton all peering back at Ruth #7 and myself.

"What are you doing here?" Emma pointed at me angrily. She turned to Sara and exclaimed, "I told you he was involved."

Milton looked first to Emma and then Grimwald and then to Hakim, asking of them all, "What are the three of you doing here?"

Emma was defiant, "Catching them in the act!" She pointed first to Ruth and then back toward me.

Elder Professor Grimwald's voice was calm, "I have been trying to ascertain just who is involved." He turned to Ruth, "It does not look good for you."

"Ruth is not guilty of changing the approved timeline!" I stated irrefutably.

Emma appeared exasperated, "What are you talking about? We just caught her. It was recorded on the Akasha!"

The Governor-General spoke, "There has got to be another answer." She looked upon each of us in turn before adding, "Aside from this situation, I do not believe Ruth is guilty. This was merely an attempt to discover who is truly responsible.

Milton chose to follow, "Someone has been changing the ATL but it is not Ruth. Unless it is one of us, the culprit did not come. Perhaps they somehow became aware of the deception we had planned?"

"The matter remains quite unclear to me," Hakim managed to say, his words causing Emma to frown.

Although Professor Grimwald appeared reluctant to speak, he chose to agree with Emma, "I am afraid that Ruth has got to be responsible. Once a Horologium is yours, it is yours. There is no way to fool the Akasha."

Through it all, Elizabeth I and William Davison spoke between themselves, completely oblivious to the seven of us present within the very same room. As I looked first to the queen and then toward Davison, I repeatedly contemplated Grimwald's statement in my head: "Once a Horologium is yours, it is yours." All at once, an idea came to mind that had never presented itself before. For the first time, I possessed clarity about the entire situation before us.

"Wait!" was all that would come forth as the thought took hold of me. "I know who is responsible, and I understand how it was done."

Although the solution was before me, I suggested that as representatives of the League the greatest issue of import was first setting right what Ruth had purposefully set wrong. It was relatively straightforward for her to revisit the matter within the queen's own mind and give thought to reconsidering the warrant's approval. By so doing, Queen Elizabeth I affixed her signature with some measure of regret and requested of Davison that if another way could be found, it be given every

consideration (even proposing the untimely murder
of Mary, if possible, before such execution could take
place). Once Davison procured the signed warrant in
hand, problems affecting timelines VI, XLII, and LXXV
were reset and quickly righted themselves within
approved ATL parameters.

Once the seven of us had returned to the League,
I asked the others for some measure of flexibility in
the issue before us. (Only Emma seemed reluctant
in granting the request and relented only upon the
Governor-General's insistence.) When Sara, Milton,
Ruth, and I were alone, I divulged what I had come to
believe, and proposed a timeline excursion involving
the four of us. I explained that we would need Sara's
approval for what was to follow:

"Miss Sara, the League Disciplinary Process states,
'Upon approval of the Governor-General anyone
suspected of a serious violation of time travel protocols
may be tracked at any time without their knowledge . . .' I
understand your Horologium has some manner of control
over such matters?"

The Governor-General nodded in acknowledgment,
explaining that her own "TEMPUS" button could be
pressed a fourth time making such possible: "Anyone
standing near me will see all that I see. Anyone at a
distance to my Horologium, however, will remain
unaware of our presence until I choose otherwise."

It was shortly thereafter that Sara, Milton, Ruth, and
I stood against the wall of a cavern not far from a place
called the Dead Sea where a group once known as the
Essenes had established themselves. Ruth had provided
us with the necessary information, as this was the
moment of her own recruitment, nearly two thousand
years before my own. I took note of the surroundings
before us:

An old woman lay upon the floor, covered with one, thin, worn blanket. She appeared frail and withered with age. The only signs that life still remained present were her erratic and shallow breathing. Scattered about the cavern was an abundance of dried grass, which served as the only comfort between her body and the hard, stone floor. Several large clay jars were scattered about containing parchment scrolls that the woman had been working upon before the pain in her body had become too severe. As we had chosen the woman as our target, her remaining thoughts came readily to mind.

As she faded in and out of consciousness she wished only that her work would continue. She knew her time was near but it was not a time she feared. She had been blessed with a very long life. So long, in fact, that her husband and her children had all passed before her. Still, she had no regrets, save one: There was so much more she wished to accomplish, if only she had the time.

We stood quietly near the stone wall, simply watching the woman in silence. Suddenly, the ghostly form of her personal recruiter began to materialize. Although his beard was shorter and appeared to be more gray than white, Emmett stood before us holding his pocket watch in one hand and the Horologium assigned to Ruth in the other. He moved toward the old woman to awaken her. Before he could speak, however, a vaporous image of his other self (with a whiter beard and longer hair) appeared before us. We could see them both, whereas our own presence remained unknown.

"I am your other self," the Emmett I knew spoke to his previous version. "I am in need of Ruth's Horologium."

Although somewhat confused by the appearance of another image of himself, the gray-haired Emmett managed to inquire, "For what purpose?"

"You have grown tired of endless experiences of the

very same work. It is a work that is never-ending. For many millennia we have toiled, and the task we chose from the first is no closer than the moment we started." The old man then added, "It was you who decided there had to be another way. I am here only to assist YOU!"

The first version of Emmett appeared to contemplate the matter before responding, "What would you ask of me?"

"Loan me her Horologium," he said, pointing to the woman on the floor. "I will leave and return in but a moment."

When his words had been spoken, Sara touched her Horologium, causing the ghostly form of the four of us to appear before them. It was the Governor-General who spoke:

"Emmett!" She exclaimed loudly, causing both versions of the old man to turn in our direction. "We know what you have been doing. We know it has been you all along. Why would you change the ATL?"

The white-haired Emmett turned to Sara and stated without remorse, "Have you not realized that our labors are without end? All we have done has come to naught."

Ruth chose to go next, "Emmett, please come back with us. I forgive you. I will recommend leniency in this matter."

The Governor-General concurred, "Yes, Emmett, there has to be a way. We have been friends for a very long time."

Emmett shook his head in defiance, "I cannot . . . I will not go back."

Milton spoke firmly, "You need to come with us!"

"I don't think so," the white-haired Emmett replied. "I am through with the League."

At the words of his older self, the younger version of Emmett appeared surprised. He looked first between the old man and Sara, and then glanced between Sara and Ruth's Horologium, which he held within his hand. He then turned to his older self and looked back at the four of us against the cavern wall.

"Give me her Horologium," the older Emmett demanded. "Give it to me quickly!"

The younger Emmett turned once again to Sara before looking toward Ruth, who stood next to her.

I had never seen Emmett angry but he spoke with much force, "Give it to me!"

"I don't think so," the younger Emmett asserted. He walked toward Ruth, placing the pocket watch within her own hands, "You need to have this."

Milton repeated his words for a second time, telling the white-haired Emmett, "You need to come with us!"

The older Emmett looked toward the four of us as he responded, "I don't think so! I will find Bruce, and Melvin, and Adda, and all those who have gone before! I have found a new calling!" He took his own Horologium in hand and a moment later disappeared.

When the fact of his departure had become clear to us, Ruth #7 turned to me and called to mind that which was of greatest import. She passed me the Horologium that she had received but a moment earlier and asserted, "Ben, I think you should do it."

It was in this manner that I became the very recruiter of the one who had recruited me. Such are the perplexities of time travel.

The complications and particulars of all that transpired since the moment of Ruth's recruitment may be too numerous to detail. Let me simply provide some semblance of summary of that which occurred thereafter:

To begin, the details of Emmett's involvement with changing the ATL were soon communicated to every member of the Core, and Ruth was returned to her honored place within the school and the League. She received apologies from all who had once believed her guilt. I can affirm with certainty, however, that Emma was not numbered among them, as she found no reason to seek forgiveness. It soon became clear that Emma, herself, regularly examined the travels of every member of the Core as a means of personally ascertaining whether or not they might be in violation of time travel protocols. (I note here that the Governor-General has vowed to establish a hearing of some nature to explore appropriate reprimands for Emma's inexcusable behavior.)

It became an ironic conclusion to understand that Emma's examinations of personal travels and timelines (and her own repeated investigations of Elizabethan history) were that which prompted Emmett to suspect these activities were being monitored. With Emmett's departure and his choice to wander through time (as those few who have gone before him), undertaking whatever desire he might imagine, at least until he can be apprehended, the Core remembered Athena's background and interest and named her the new "Keeper of the Records." I will add here that it is a promotion about which she is very enthusiastic. As much as possible, all things have the appearance of returning to some measure of normalcy.

Once our scheduled curriculum resumed, Agnes #23 provided an occasion for Bonne Souer Marie, Emanuel, and me to give some semblance of accounting of our most recent mission assignments. I gave details of the experience I encountered and Ruth's own involvement in the matter of Elizabeth I, which she promptly reset to ATL parameters. Emanuel provided a thorough assessment of how changes within the Anglican and Catholic Churches had been righted, and how the two faiths would remain separate but nearly identical for at least some time to come. Bonne Souer Marie delivered a moving account of her own activities with healing and helping many heal themselves as a senseless war waged upon the open seas and near the coastlines of two strong and stubbornly opposed countries.

When the three of us had finished our individual deliberations and Agnes was near unto rising from her seat to begin anew our scheduled curriculum, my roomie called attention to himself by waving his arm throughout the air.

Our instructress pointed in his direction and inquired, "Yes, George #111. What is it?"

He stood and proceeded to walk toward the front of the class, "I am ready to give details of the mission that Manuela and I rectified between us."

Agnes was very much surprised, "What mission? I don't remember a mission for the two of you!"

"It came directly from the ATL Mission Office," George spoke with certainty.

Although Agnes #23 appeared filled with some measure of confusion, she sat back down and motioned for him to proceed.

George took the stylus from the desk and wrote two words on the board as they were spoken aloud: "Roanoke Island." Perhaps as a means of acquiring appropriate credit, he underlined them twice and looked in our teacher's direction to make certain she had taken occasion to make note of such.

"When Elizabeth I realized there would be an attack from the Spanish Armada, all voyages, and excursions beyond the shores of England were immediately canceled. To assure its own protection, Britain needed to retain its resources at home. When this occurred, problems were created on multiple timelines, especially timelines LIV and XC, which Manuela and I found to be the most prominent." George pointed toward Manuela #64 as she nodded in agreement. He continued, "You see, the colony on Roanoke Island was in desperate need of supplies, and when the queen impounded all ships, it led to a major disaster for the colonists, as there would be no ships coming from England."

My roomie proceeded to describe how on various timelines two years of drought and harsh winters had brought sickness and death to the colonists until those who had made the journey to the New World were no more. He then called upon Manuela to describe the harsh conditions experienced by the colonists and what the two had done to rectify the issue:

"George and I agreed that the best course of action was to revisit the colony before the disaster and have the Indians take the colonists in as their own. As the Croatan Indians had shown much kindness previously, we influenced the Croatan Chief and a few others to do just that. The colonists agreed to abandon Roanoke Island and follow the Indians in their migration to the south."

My roomie added, "We encouraged the colonists to carve the word 'CROATAN' on one of the posts near the fort they were leaving behind. In that way, if anyone ever returned from England they would know who had taken them in."

Manuela finished by concluding, "In time, the colonists intermingled with the Indians and lived out the remainder of their lives. The ATL disaster was rectified on the timelines we had chosen to fix." Her conclusion was simply, "The end."

Once we had applauded our approval and George and Manuela had retaken their seats, Agnes #23 returned to the front of the class (still appearing somewhat confused). Nevertheless, a moment later she pulled a folded piece of paper from her pocket, unfolded it before us, and began reading from the most recent mission assignment list:

"Ben #239, destination Cuzco, Peru, 1114, in the matter of Sapa Inca and his creation of the Inca Empire."

"Bonne Souer Marie #304, destination Harvard University, Cambridge, Massachusetts, 1886, in the matter of Dr. Reginald Heber Fitz and his work with appendectomies."

"Emanuel #41, destination Kansas City, Missouri, 1889, in the matter of Charles and Myrtle Fillmore and their establishment of Unity Church Headquarters."

"George #111, destination Athens, Greece, 143, in the matter of Herodes and Regilla Atticus, and their efforts as benefactors of the Grecian empire."

"Manuela #64, destination Seoul, Korea, 2063, in the matter of the people's reunification of the Korean peninsula."

Agnes resumed her bobbing about as she waved the pages in her hand before us, "I highly recommend you go to the Akasha to get the background information you will need for these assignments. If you need any help, ask Athena #56. Athena knows everything! Class dismissed!"

As the five of us walked down the first hallway leading to the Akasha library, I turned to my roomie and asked, "Did you really get that assignment from the ATL Mission Office?"

George grinned before speaking, "Let me simply say that Manuela and I went to Athena and asked her if saving the colonists would cause any problems along the approved timeline. When she saw only a minor ripple in history, we decided to proceed with the mission assignment."

I nodded in agreement, "Maybe you have found a new type of mission where you can best use your talents? Those that only cause a minor ripple in history."

"Maybe," my roomie agreed wholeheartedly.

It was later that evening, once I had finished my own research and after Athena had helped a few others with information on their next destinations, that I stood in the center of the library and waited as she walked toward me. She smiled, and after making certain we were alone, I leaned forward and gave her a very long kiss.

"I have missed you," I said softly.

Athena nodded in agreement and asked, "Do you want to go somewhere where we can be alone?" She pulled her Horologium from her pocket, smiling as she held it before me, "We have all the time in the world."

A Note to Readers:

Many aspects of the historical incidents detailed within *A Time Traveler's Journal* are true, beginning with the fact that the Treaty of Kadesh is considered the first peace treaty in history.

The Moberly-Jourdain time slip, Victor Goddard's time slip, and the Medieval time slip are all regarded as the most genuine time slips on record.

As to the accuracy of Asahi's April time slip in the year 2248, only time will tell.

Made in the USA
Middletown, DE
17 May 2022

65825854R00115